Gimme a Gangsta

The Patton Brothers
Book 2

K.L. Hall

B. Love Publications

Gimme a Gangsta Synopsis

First rule of spinning the block with your ex after two years?
Never catch feelings for the bad boy who shattered your heart.
Rule number two?
Definitely don't get pregnant.

I've spent the last couple of years finding adventure in the friendly skies, bouncing from one city to the next without a care in the world. That is until a twist of fate, in the form of some unexpected turbulence, thrusts me right into my ex's arms while working the first-class cabin.
Despite the time gap, Amir Patton still melts my insides like Superman.
And after an emergency landing, an overnight layover, and a few drinks at the bar, let's just say he's got my legs spread like Nutella on toast.

When the sun rises, I know better than to make the same mistake twice.
I won't get involved long term.

But when the stick turns pink a few weeks later, the situation
escalates to a whole new level of complexity.
Being in Amir's presence has me tipsy on a cocktail of emotions.
There's still so much of me that resents the player he used to be, but
our child deserves a father.
How long can I keep my heart hidden behind the wall I've built,
especially when the only weakness I've ever had is him?

Amir Patton

hree weeks later.

THE BASS THUMPED LOUDLY, VIBRATING THE WALLS OF THE Vegas nightclub. It was popping with energy and good vibes. I stood at the center of it all, surrounded by Ahsan, Sienna, and XL. We were gathered in the VIP section, a sectioned-off area with black leather sofas, bottles on bottles of liquor, and an excellent view of every baddie shaking ass on the dance floor.

"Can you believe this shit, nigga?" I yelled to Ahsan and XL over the music. "We're finally here. You with your real estate shit, XL about to open up his restaurant on that land you bought, and me, well... you already know what I'm celebrating." I raised my shot glass. "This is for every late night, every deal, every risk we ever took, and for any nigga who was dumb enough to try and stop us!"

Ahsan chuckled. "Hell yeah! Big Mama would be proud of her boys."

"Hey, let's not get too sentimental now. We don't want motha-fuckas crying in the club. We're here to celebrate, right? To Amir, one of the coldest Patton niggas alive!" XL added.

Everyone raised their shot glasses, and a chorus of clinking glasses rang out as we cheered.

"Now, let's get this mothafuckin party started!" I cheered.

I grabbed a bottle of champagne, popped the cork off, and watched fizz spray all over the table as my niggas cheered around me. I poured the champagne for everyone, and our group toasted once more before I took the rest of the bottle to the head.

As the night stretched, the neon-lit place buzzed with baddies trying to get into our section. Ahsan and Sienna kept the birds away while I was on the dance floor, moving to the rhythm in a carefree mood while getting twerked on. Suddenly, the vibe shifted when I felt a firm tap on my shoulder. My head swiveled with the snap of my neck to see Brandi, my fiancée, standing there with her gang of girls in tow.

Her skin was golden beige with a red undertone, a testament to her mixed Puerto Rican and African American roots. Her long, jet-black hair was bone-straight and parted down the middle, cascading down to the tip of her ass. As much attitude as Brandi had, she had an ass built for back shots and a mouth made for sucking. Her perky C-cup chest sat high underneath her white button-up shirt with a gold Chanel brooch pinned over her right breast. A black, pleated miniskirt with a gold-chained Gucci belt hugged her slim waist, and the hem barely covered the cuff of her ass. She accentuated her look with the gold Louis Vuitton hoop earrings I'd bought her for her birthday and black heels with gold Cuban link accents over the open-toe and heel.

Her eyes narrowed onto mine, and her expression hardened to stone. It was evident from her furrowed brows and the tight line of her full lips that she hadn't expected to see what had unfolded in front of her eyes, her nigga getting backed down by a bad bitch in the middle of the dance floor. I just wanted to have a good time and let loose with my family without her drama. But she looked like she was ready to start World War III. *This shit can't be happening. Not tonight.*

Brandi smacked her full, glossy lips. "Having fun, I see," she snapped.

The festive mood surrounding me and the D'USSÉ in my system was no match for the icy tension her presence brought with it.

"Baby? What are you doing here? I thought you were having a girls' night out."

She scoffed. "Don't baby me, nigga. We were having a good time until I got on IG and saw your little celebration. Who the fuck is this?" she yelled, gesturing to the woman I had been dancing with.

"Oh, she's just—"

Brandi cut me off with the wave of her long, stiletto-shaped nails. "Save that shit, nigga! I can't believe you up in here embarrassing me and shit!"

The music faded to the background as the tension between us stacked like Jenga pieces. I looked across the dance floor to see my family watching from the VIP booth with concern. They watched with bated breath, hoping we wouldn't cause a scene, something we'd been known to do. *I can't let this shit escalate. I've got to keep it together for the family and the business.*

I huffed before reaching out to grab her hand. "C'mon, baby. Let's talk about this outside."

She snatched her hand away. "Nigga, don't touch me! It's obvious you can't keep your hands off bum broke-ass hos! I don't want the secondhand filth."

The woman I'd been dancing with barked back. "What the fuck you say, bitch? Because you talking like you can beat me up, and I don't like that shit!"

My aggravation emerged, swallowing my faded, jovial mood whole. I felt the rumblings of a growing storm brewing. I'd never seen Brandi fight, but she sure talked a hell of a lot of shit. I snatched up Brandi by her wrist, forcing her to look me in the eyes.

"Come on, Brandi. Don't piss me the fuck off tonight, all right? Just bring your ass outside so we can talk about this shit like some mothafuckin adults!" I barked.

"Fuck you, nigga! Move out of my way! Got these bum-ass, file cabinet-built bitches wishing they were me! Up in here embarrassing me and shit! Got me finding out about my nigga's whereabouts on social media like some groupie ho! What? Am I a fan now like these bitches? Nigga got me fucked up!"

Brandi continued to argue with herself as we made our way through the crowd and headed toward the exit. We stepped outside the club into the dry night air. The muffled sounds of the bass faded behind us as we faced each other. She hit me with a fiery look that said she was ready to lock my ass up with no trial.

"What the fuck is up with you coming in there talking all that shit like you crazy!" I barked, letting off first.

"Spare me, nigga! Is that who you been fucking on?"

"Fucking on? I'm not fucking on nobody but you, Brandi, and you know that!"

"Yeah, okay. Ever since you proposed, your ass has been on one. What the fuck else am I supposed to think?"

"Just because I'm busy doesn't mean I'm fucking around. The two don't equate."

She scoffed. "Don't play like you're Mr. Innocent, Amir. You know what you are? You're an unstable creature!"

"And you're toxic as hell! The shit that comes out of your mouth ain't got no logic behind it whatsoever. You just want to have a reason to be mad so I'll fuck that attitude right out of you! I know your patterns, Brandi. I know you feel a way when I'm out late. I know you pick fights about dumb ass shit when you're bored. This shit ain't nothing new."

"You think this is about dick, nigga? I've been calling and chasing you all day, Amir. Then I had to find out where you were online, only to pop up and see you in here with some ho? How the fuck is that supposed to make me feel as your fiancée?"

I sighed. "Listen, I know how it looked in there, but it wasn't what you think. It was just a dance. I didn't get the bitch name, number, zodiac sign, next of kin, or nothing."

She folded her arms across her busty chest. "It's not just about the fucking dance, Amir. It's about us, our future, and the fact that you still don't know how to treat me even after putting a goddamn ring on my finger. If I'm going to be your wife, I need to know we're on the same page, let alone the same book."

"We are. How many times I gotta tell you that? It don't matter how many karats I put on your finger, how many designer bags I put on your arm, or the clothes I put on your back. You stay letting your insecurities eat your ass alive, and that's not my problem. It's yours!"

We'd been at each other's throats more than usual for a couple like us. She'd become a full-time bridezilla ever since I proposed, which came with its own set of issues, and she'd only had the ring on her finger for a few months. Any discussions about wedding planning had become a sensitive subject. Hell, any discussions about anything seemed to trigger her hostile ass. It didn't matter what I said. She already had her mind made up that she wanted to be mad, logic be damned.

She rolled her eyes toward the night sky. "I don't even see the point in repeating myself, because I already know you won't listen! Just take me home!"

INSIDE THE CAR, A HEAVY SILENCE HUNG IN THE AIR. I COULDN'T believe her ass had the audacity to show up at the club and cause a scene like that. She only felt comfortable popping off like that because she knew I was right there to break up anything before it went too far. After almost a year and a half of being together, I shouldn't have been surprised. Brandi had been a fiery hothead since the day I met her. I learned long ago that Brandi's dramatic nature was a part of who she was, and I accepted her for it. She needed to be the center of attention; most times, I was happy to spotlight her. But it was the overwhelming moments where I felt like I was walking on a tightrope trying to balance my need for peace with her chaos. Most days, I still couldn't believe I'd gotten down on one knee and proposed. Whenever she acted out with one of her temper tantrums, I became unsure about meeting her at the altar. But, since she was aware of my lifestyle and had been loyal, I kept rocking with her.

On one hand, I was drawn to the spice and intensity that Brandi's overly dramatic personality brought to my life. Her dramatic, attention-seeking ways added an element of unpredictability that almost always led to bomb-ass head or sex. However, that same passion was like a double-edged sword. Navigating the highs and lows of Brandi's theatrics was emotionally draining. I often longed for something less stressful and calm—the opposite of my everyday life and relationship with her.

I sucked my teeth. "I can't believe your ass showed up in the club like that. You lucky that girl ain't try to beat your ass."

Her brows downturned. "Beat who ass? Not mine."

"Regardless, you gotta stop popping off like that in public, Brandi. That shit ain't cute, especially when you walking around with my ring on your finger."

"Whatever, nigga. I did what I did, and I'd do it again."

"Yeah, all right. Keep playing. Your mouth gon' fuck around and write a check your ass can't afford to cash," I warned.

She folded her arms across her chest as her neck whipped sideways. "So you'd let a bitch put her hands on me, Amir?"

I released a stifled breath. "That's not what I'm saying, Brandi."

"Then what the fuck are you saying, Amir? Because I thought I said yes to marrying a real nigga who'd have my back, period. Am I wrong?"

"Forreal, Brandi, you getting on my mothafuckin nerves with all that shit. When have I ever let anybody say or do anything to you? Huh? Never. And you know it, so shut the fuck up with that shit."

"Nigga, who the fuck do you think you're talking to? I may be wearing your ring, but all that can change real quick."

My brow furrowed. "Choose your next words carefully, Brandi."

"Fuck you, Amir! You don't give a damn about none of my time anyway. Why the fuck would I sign up to live that way for the rest of my life?"

"The fuck are you saying?" I queried, a storm of confusion brewing in my gaze.

"I'm saying I feel trapped!"

"Trapped? Ain't nobody keeping your ass where you don't wanna be kept."

She smacked her full lips. "Not like that. I love you, I do, but love shouldn't be this hard."

"It's only this hard because you're making it that way. It was just one fucking dance, Brandi. Come on, yo! Stop with the dramatics."

"It's not just one thing; it's a thousand little things that tell me we don't need to be doing this shit, Amir. You're obviously not ready to be a husband."

"If I weren't ready, I wouldn't have asked you in the fucking first place!" I spat, deep down, knowing the truth.

"Then act like it, or I'll find a nigga who will!"

"Let's get one thing straight. Ain't no way I'ma let you threaten to fuck on another mothafucka while wearing my ring, not in this lifetime or the next."

She slipped the ring off her finger and tossed it in my lap. "No ring, no problem, right?"

I sat in stunned silence, momentarily paralyzed by the shock. Once a symbol of my love and commitment, the engagement ring lay abandoned in my lap, sparkling under the streetlight. My mind galloped to catch up with the suddenness of her emotion-driven actions. Brandi was trying to show me which of us had the bigger balls. She underestimated the fact that I loved a challenge. A flash of anger washed over my face as I pulled over and brought the car to a halt.

"Since it's clear you don't need me, get the fuck out."

Her brows bunched low. "Excuse me?"

I put the car in park and unlocked the doors. "You wanna leave? Go ahead and leave!"

"Amir!"

"Get the fuck out of the car, Brandi. I'm not repeating myself."

Brandi's face dropped as abruptly as the ring fell in my lap. A range of emotions crossed her face, from confusion and sadness to anger. Her brown orbs widened, and her mouth opened slightly as she processed the sudden, intense change of events.

"Fine! You think a bitch like me needs a fickle ass nigga like you? I don't! I know my worth!" she screamed before shoving me upside my temple and unhooking her seat belt.

Brandi exited my Range Rover with a huff and slammed my fucking door so hard the windshield rattled.

I quickly rolled the automatic window down. "Don't slam my mothafuckin door!"

"Fuck you and your door, nigga!" Brandi yelled back before storming down the street with her fingernails tapping away at her phone screen.

I sat motionless, the shock rooting me to the driver's seat. I understood emotionally-driven decisions. I'd made a few a time or two. Brandi's emotions had driven her to make the choice that felt right in the moment, and so did mine. I knew I shouldn't have kicked her out, but I felt wildly disrespected. Her savage spontaneity was a gift and a curse, sexy as hell, yet detrimental as a mothafucka when planning for the long term.

My Range Rover's engine hummed as I rolled slowly beside the sidewalk. I glanced around. The night's darkness and the sidewalk's emptiness heightened my protective instincts. No matter how pissed off I was, I didn't want her to be alone in an unsafe environment.

I leaned over the passenger seat, calling out to Brandi. "C'mon, Brandi. Get in the car, all right? It's late, and you know it's not safe for you to be walking alone."

Brandi carried herself off, refusing to break her stride. She clutched her phone tightly while glancing at me with annoyance. "I don't need a ride from you, nigga. I've got one coming."

"C'mon, baby. You win. I just want you to be safe."

"I can take care of myself! I'm waiting for my Uber. I don't need you to fucking protect me!"

I sighed, the lines etched on my forehead deepening. "Fuck it, B. If you say you good, then be good."

I watched her from my rearview mirror with an ache prowling about my ribs as I pulled off, frustrated because I couldn't convince her to see things from my perspective. Big Mama always said life required balance between the head and the heart, and Brandi's impulsive ass didn't have an ounce of foresight. I grunted, knowing she would be the downfall of our future together.

———

BACK AT HOME, MY MIND ECHOED WITH CONCERN AS I WAITED for Brandi. I sat on the couch in a state of restless anticipation. Lost in thought, I reflected on my relationship with Brandi and the uncertainty of our future together. Memories of my birthday party and my proposal flooded my mind. It was like I was outside my body, watching some other nigga bend the knee. The nervousness in my voice as the words *'Will you marry me?'* falling off my tongue felt like someone else should've been saying them. Yet, there I was, diamond ring in hand, looking up at her. The sparkle of tears in Brandi's eyes when she said yes to becoming my wife felt like a dream. A dream that had somehow turned into a nightmare I wasn't sure I could wake up from.

Overall, I rocked with Brandi. She'd been there for me through thick and thin. She was my ride-or-die. There was no doubt about that. But was that enough to build forever on? Loyalty like hers was rare, but it did come with its share of unpleasant trade-offs. *What the fuck did I get myself into? Marriage means forever, right?* I kept asking myself was I going through with it because it was right or because it was expected. Because she deserved it, or because I owed it to her.

I slid my hand in my pocket and pulled out the ring. She'd given it back, which, in my eyes, meant we were done. A part of me looked at it like a blessing in disguise. My heart and mind were in a game of tug-of-war over making a life-changing decision based on obligation rather than actual desire. My love for Brandi was undeniable, but so were my doubts about marrying her unpredictable ass.

I found my feet, trying to distract myself in her absence, but time seemed to crawl. I checked my phone every few minutes, each passing second stretching on longer than the last. Occasionally, I caught myself pacing the length of the living room. Finally, after what felt like an eternity, she arrived two hours later. Relief washed over me immediately, content with knowing she was safe.

I approached her, my steps minced. "Baby, I'm glad you're home."

Brandi scoffed while kicking off her heels at the door. "No thanks to your ass."

"Where have you been? It's been two hours. I was worried about you."

She scoffed while rolling her eyes skyward. "Worried? Just like a man to miss a good thing when it's gone. Don't start giving a fuck about me now that we not together."

I sighed. "Chill with the rah-rah shit, all right? I'm not trying to argue with your ass anymore. You know I love you, Brandi. I'm sorry for making you feel otherwise."

Her expression softened as she uncrossed her arms. "I want to believe you, Amir. I do. But with you taking over the business and all these changes... I just feel left out. It's like I'm only getting half of you."

I reached out for her hand. "I never meant to make you feel that way, baby. How about this? Tomorrow, we'll talk about everything: the wedding plans, the business, and us. I want you to be a part of it all."

She nodded. "I'd like that. I just want us to be a team, you know?"

"We are a team. Tonight was supposed to be about celebrating success, but none of it means shit without you. Nothing is more important to me than our future."

Brandi flashed a crinkle of a smile and crashed into my arms. I instantly felt the negativity between us dissipating. "You waited up for me?" she asked, hooking her arms around my waist.

My hands inched from her waist to her juicy ass before giving it a squeeze. "You know I can't sleep unless you're next to me, girl."

I buried my face in her neck, and she giggled while squirming underneath my grasp. My dick pulsed, ready to feel her body up under mine. One thing was for sure, Brandi's attitude may have been venomous, but her pussy was heaven sent.

Nerissa "Rizzy" Barnes

The plane landed, and I stood by the door, bidding farewell to the stream of passengers as they disembarked.

"Thank you for flying with us. Enjoy your stay in Vegas!" I beamed, my voice cheery and upbeat.

I loved the sense of freedom that came with being a flight attendant. The opportunity to travel domestically and abroad, meet new people, and experience different cultures firsthand was precisely what I needed to overcome my heartbreak and find myself again. At thirty-five thousand feet in the air, no two shifts were the same.

Aside from that, I appreciated the flexibility in my schedule. While the hours could be irregular, they also allowed me to make the most of my days off, pursuing my career as a traveling hairstylist. Whether it was a classic blowout or booty-length box braids, I loved making every client feel confident and glamorous. My dual careers allowed me to merge my love for travel with my passion for hairstyling and make enough money to take care of myself. As a traveling stylist, I offered my services to clients around the country, coordinating with my flight schedule to meet the needs of my clientele.

I stepped off the plane into the jet bridge. The sounds of slot machines and distant cheers echoed through the airport walls. I paused as the side of my mouth lifted on one side. I pulled out my phone and sent a swift message to my younger brother, Maree.

Me: *Landed safe in Vegas. See you for dinner in a few.*

I wheeled my carry-on down the corridor, eager to get to my hotel and change before meeting him for dinner. I left Vegas two and a half years ago when he was in prison. We were half-siblings with the same father and different mothers. We didn't grow up under the same roof and weren't very close, but blood was blood. I still loved him and looked forward to seeing him after so long.

HOURS LATER, I SAT AT A TABLE FOR TWO IN THE RESTAURANT inside my hotel on the Strip. I checked the time on my phone for the third time, my leg bouncing impatiently. *His ass is late again. It's always the same story.* I took a sip of water as my eyes scanned the crowd. I was hopeful yet skeptical about his arrival. The years of letdowns were a dark shadow over my optimism. I texted him.

Me: *Where are you, Maree? I don't have all night.*

My message received no immediate response. My growing annoyance was visible. While in town, I could've met with a client and made some quick cash, but I blocked off my schedule for the evening to spend time with him.

I found myself glancing at my phone more often than I cared to admit. Each vibration raised my hopes, only to be met with irrelevant notifications. It was a raging cycle of hope and letdown, a pattern that had become all too familiar in my interactions with him throughout my entire life.

As the minutes ticked by, my mind wandered to our childhood. We weren't the closest of siblings. I could count on one hand the number of holidays we spent together growing up. But there were some good times before life pulled us in different directions—him to the streets and me toward my dream of traveling and doing hair. I remembered his laughter and how he made me feel so overprotective of him as his big sister. Despite my annoyance, I couldn't help but hold on to hope that he'd come through. Although I rarely mentioned having a sibling to people, without our father around to fill the void, I missed having my brother in my life.

While waiting for my brother, I ordered something light from the menu. I opted for a few spring rolls and a lemonade, nothing too heavy. I still wanted to enjoy a real meal once he arrived. My phone buzzed. It was him, finally.

Bro: *Running late, got caught up in traffic. Don't leave. Be there in ten. I promise.*

I rolled my eyes, a dry smirk lifting one corner of my lips as I sighed. *This nigga stays with the excuses, but at least he's on the way.*

My eyes drifted back and forth from my phone to the entrance. Another twenty minutes passed before he arrived. Maree stood there, his stature taller and amber brown locs longer than I remembered. He'd matured. His presence was commanding yet subtle. He paused, eyes scanning the room for me. Our eyes locked as I waved him over. He flashed me a heartfelt grin, the kind that seemed like it hadn't graced his features since we were kids. A warmth I hadn't felt in years spread through me like sunshine.

I shot to my feet to greet him. "Maree!"

He grinned with all his teeth as he approached the table and hugged me. "Hey, Rizzy. You look amazing, big sis. I like the hair."

I ran my hand over my head, full of voluminous wand curls. "Thank you. You look good yourself!"

My eyes traveled over his ruggedly handsome caramel face—from his heavy-lidded whiskey eyes to his coily beard and the tattoos inked up his neck, arms, and collarbone.

"Thank you!"

"So, c'mon, sit down. Tell me what's been up with you. Five years is a long time."

"Tell me about it."

"I'm proud of you for keeping your head up in there. But what's next for you? We both know the streets aren't kind."

He dipped his chin. "I know. I got plans though."

"Like what? I mean, what I'm really trying to hear you say is, that life is behind you."

"I can't say that, but what I can say is I've been working on a business plan."

"What kind of business plan, Demario?" I queried, calling him by his government name. "You ain't getting no younger. What about settling down with a good girl, having a couple of kids, and building a life you can be proud of?" I suggested.

He scoffed. "That love shit is behind me. I tried fixing things with the girl I was with back when I went in, but she ain't trying to hear all that."

"So, move on and find someone else. Someone who will be good at keeping you on the right path and not back in the game."

Demario sucked his teeth. "I didn't come here for a lecture."

"And I didn't come here to give one."

"You don't get it. The game is all a nigga know, Rizzy. You can't blame me for wanting to get back to my roots. Things are more complicated now without a connect, but I'm planning to get my footing back in the game. I've already got a little plan in motion."

I frowned, not hearing the answer I wanted to. My concern for my brother's well-being only grew more intense. I knew a scheme when I heard one, and I wanted no part of whatever get rich quick venture he was conspiring. "So, what you're telling me is you've learned nothing in five years. It's like you're on a loop, making the same stupid mistakes."

"Things are going to be different this time around. I can feel it."

His baseless assurances did nothing to settle the butterflies tormenting my gut. "Do you know how lucky you are to get a second chance? I hate to see you throw your life away on bullshit."

Demario shifted uncomfortably, his bouncing gaze avoiding mine. "I know. It's just—"

I interrupted him, my tone firm. "No, listen to me. A lot happened while you were away," I said, thinking about the passing of our father. "And I promised Dad that I'd...I don't want to watch you spiral down the wrong path again, okay? I can't stand by and not say anything now that Dad's gone and not here to tell you himself."

"I get it, I do. And I'm sorry about not being there when he got sick and not getting a prison furlough for his funeral, all right? It's just hard when the game has its claws in you, you know? But I'm doing things right this time."

My expression softened. I knew I was fighting a losing battle. We were going to have to agree to disagree on his lifestyle choices. After all, he was his own man, and I damn sure wasn't his mother.

After catching up over dinner and drinks, the night winded down. We stood outside the restaurant.

"Listen, I have an early flight, but this... this was great. I'm glad we finally got to catch up. Stay out of trouble while I'm gone, okay?"

"It was, Rizzy. And hey, I'm good. I'll be around. No more disappearing acts from me," he promised, hugging me again. "A nigga is *never* going back to jail."

Amir

Inside the dimly lit pool hall, I leaned against the table, cue in hand. My gaze drifted off to clacking billiard balls smacking against each other before sailing into the pockets. Ahsan and XL crowded around me, sensing my thoughts were elsewhere.

"Nigga, what's on your mind?" Ahsan asked, chalking his cue stick.

I sighed, the sound almost lost in the bass-heavy track playing through the speakers. "It's about Brandi, yo. She gave me back the ring after we left the club last week."

Ahsan raised an eyebrow. "You feelin' a way about that shit?"

XL smacked his lips. "He gotta be, nigga. Look at him, face longer than a basset hound's."

They both had a quick chuckle at my expense. "Fuck both of y'all," I retorted before leaning over the table to take my next shot. "But, I don't know. This shit is confusing as fuck. We made up the same night. It was like nothing happened."

"She wearing the ring again?" Ahsan queried.

"No. We ain't really talked about what it all means, just been sweeping shit under the rug like usual. We said we were gon' talk about shit, but we didn't."

"What did y'all do then?"

"Fuck... a lot."

XL chuckled while lining up his shot. The click of the ball was sharp as it whizzed across the felt. "Sounds like you're in a gray area to me, nigga."

I nodded. "Yeah. I love her crazy ass, no doubt. Plus, the pussy is sensational. But if we're meant to be, why all this uncertainty? She was right about one thing: Being together shouldn't be this hard."

Ahsan rested his hand on my shoulder. "Maybe it's a sign. Maybe you rushed into this. Better you figured it out now than when your ass is standing at the altar."

"He's right about that. You gotta figure out if this is really what you want. Both of y'all."

"Compatibility is about more than good pussy, nigga," my brother added.

I let out a soft chuckle. "But you know good pussy will bring a nigga to his knees. Besides, the one I truly wanted got away, remember? Brandi's a ride-or-die, but part of me wonders if I'm just trying to fill that void of fucking things up with Nerissa a couple of years ago."

"You don't marry a female because you wanna keep fucking her. You marry her because you can't live without her."

"Ahsan's right, nigga. You can't marry somebody on a maybe," XL interjected, sinking another ball into the corner pocket. "Clear the air and get some clarity behind y'all relationship shit. You single or what?"

"Are you even still down to get married?" Ahsan quizzed.

I shrugged. "I mean, yeah. I am. I just gotta know if she's on the same page. As fly as I am, a nigga can't marry himself."

XL nodded. "You're right about that."

"Fuck it. I'll talk to her and figure out where we stand. No more gray areas, and hopefully, no more fucking arguments either."

Ahsan scoffed. "With Brandi? Don't hold your breath, nigga."

As the night wore on, we played game after game—the weight of 'what if' lingering heavy in the air. Bringing up Nerissa had brought thoughts of her to the forefront of my mind. She was my first and only serious relationship before I met Brandi. Nerissa, or Rizzy as I called her, was always my sunshine on a cloudy day. Her bubbly laughter was contagious, and her ambition knew no bounds. We used to spend hours vibing about life and our dreams. She wanted to become a flight attendant and meet new people, while responsibilities in the streets anchored me to Vegas.

A few weeks into her training, she broke up with me after catching me in my apartment with another female. I promised her I would do better and change, a promise that remained unfulfilled since she'd left Vegas a little over two years prior. Life moved on. After some growing up, I found love again with Brandi, but the memories of Nerissa never left the back of my mind. Sometimes, I wondered what could have been if things were different... if I had been different or fought harder to keep her, even when I knew I didn't deserve her.

I'd randomly tried looking her up online about six months back, when Brandi and I were going through one of our breakups, ready to show her I'd changed. But I couldn't find her. Without a window into her digital life, our story had become an unfinished chapter in my mind. I wondered where the friendly skies had taken her and whether she had ever looked down over Vegas and thought of me. Mostly, I missed our effortless connection. Rizzy was the only person I could communicate with without saying a damn thing. Our silence was never awkward. It was almost as if we could read each other's minds without trying.

"You know," I said, halfway lost in thoughts I shouldn't have been in, "I want what you've got with Sienna. Some peace when I walk through the door at the end of the day."

My brother laughed while lining up his shot. "Peace? Nigga, you think it's all relaxing nights and candle-lit dinners? You forget her love for art? Paint is everywhere, all the time. I'm talking tubes scattered across the floor and brushes soaking in my damn coffee mugs."

The three of us erupted in laughter as the pool balls zoomed across the green table.

"All right, you right," I conceded with a chuckle. "But at least you found something real that you ain't gotta question. And for that, you owe me. If it weren't for that bet, you wouldn't have been forced to own the feelings I knew you had since you came into the office that morning, all giddy talking about her. It's only right you name your firstborn after me. I'll settle for Amira if it's a girl."

Ahsan laughed. "Man, can you imagine being an uncle?"

I cheesed. "Hell yeah. I'ma be the fun-ass uncle too. The one who sneaks them all the extra candy and good snacks y'all say they can't have," I forewarned with a sly grin.

Sharing a humorous moment amidst the fear burning a trail to my heart felt good.

Ahsan patted my shoulder. "One day, bruh. One day."

THE THREE OF US LEANED AGAINST THE BAR AS THE EVENING started to wind down. My mind drifted to my upcoming trip to Mexico. Sure, it was a business trip, but more importantly, it was a chance to clear my head. I planned to meet with Jefe at his villa in Puerto Vallarta to inform him of the business changes from Ahsan's hands to mine. Once that was done, I planned to try to rest on the warm beaches and reset my mind. Then, I would stop in Houston on the trip back to check in on production there.

"My flight to Mexico leaves tomorrow afternoon," I informed them before tossing back a shot. "And on the way back, I'm stopping in Houston to check in on the business and see how things are moving with the expansion through Texas."

Ahsan dipped his chin. "Good. Plus, getting away and having a little space might give you the clarity you need. Sometimes, you need to distance yourself to see shit clearer."

XL nodded. "He's right. And who knows, maybe your yellow ass will come back with a tan, a suitcase full of tequila, and knowing exactly what you want."

"Life is too short for maybes and what-ifs," my brother added.

"I tell you what, come by the shop and let me line you up, get you fresh," XL offered. "Head to Mexico and handle your business, then spend the next twenty-four hours focusing on you. But seriously, nigga. *Don't* forget that tequila."

Nerissa

I was working in the first-class cabin of a commercial airliner, cruising at thirty-five thousand feet in the air on a cross-country flight from LAX to JFK. The familiar hum of the engines was a soothing backdrop to the sleeping passengers. I eased through the first-class cabin, checking on the awake passengers with an experienced eye. I paused by my co-worker Eric, who was mixing alcoholic beverages on a cart.

"Hey, you good?" I asked him.

"I'm straight. You got anything fun lined up for our layover in New York?"

I shot him a wry smile while tucking a stray lock of hair behind my left ear. "Actually, I have an appointment for a wig installation with a client. It's how I make extra cash on the side."

"Oh, that's too bad," he said with a hint of disappointment. "A few of us on the crew planned to check out this new rooftop bar in Manhattan. You sure you can't slide through and join us?"

"I appreciate the invite, but my client's been on the books for weeks. Can I get a rain check?"

"Of course! We'll paint the town red next time. You go on and make that money, darlin'!" he replied, his southern accent loud and proud.

As I walked away, my thoughts drifted to the past. No matter how many cities I'd seen or hours I'd soared, a part of me remained anchored to Vegas, my hometown. Two and a half years had passed since I moved away, yet the shadow of the man who once held the key to my heart still lingered, making every new encounter I had with someone feel like a waste of time.

Flashes of the last few years shot past my mind. I thought about the strength it took to navigate through the pieces of my crushed heart. Between flying and doing hair, I'd built a life I was proud of, where I didn't need a man to complete me. Or so I told myself. Yet, in my fragments of peace between takeoff and landing, I couldn't help but wonder if I'd ever find someone who could make my chest tighten with the same intensity as Amir Patton.

I used to be head over heels in love with everything about that man, from how he commanded a room without saying a word to the safety I felt whenever he held me in his arms. We were of the same vein. When he moved, so did I. If I were hurt, he would bleed. We were together, lost in love with each other, for two years before I discovered the truth about his infidelity. I was almost through my eight-week flight attendant training when I flew in a day early to surprise him at his apartment. Only I was the one who was surprised when I inserted my spare key.

The door creaked open, revealing an unexpected and gut-wrenching scene. The living room was dimly lit, aglow with the soft light from the TV. And there, on the couch, was Amir with his head leaned back, his chin in a euphoric tilt, while a bitch bobbed up and down on his dick. My breath hitched, the shock sending a suffocating blow to my chest. The moaning and slurping that filled the room fell silent as if the entire world paused.

"W-what the f-fuck?" I yelled, wrinkled lines crowding my forehead.

Amir shot up to his feet, his brow a thundercloud. The surprised look on his face would forever be carved into my memory. Time seemed to stretch on forever as I stood there, the radiating pain in my chest growing with each thunderous thump of my shattered heart. He raced to pull up his jeans from around his ankles as the naked bitch on her knees hurried to get dressed.

I studied the whore. She was tall and slender, with a sense of entitlement that seemed to hang over her like a dark cloud. Her long braids cascaded over her shoulders, framing her brown face, which was a five at best. Her icy gaze held a calculated glimmer as they settled on mine, showing no hint of remorse for her scheming actions no matter how quickly her limbs moved. It was as if she were staking her silent claim on *my* man. It spoke louder than words ever could. At that moment, I understood that the bitch wasn't a one-off. She was a choice that he'd made on more than one occasion, not giving a fuck about the heartache his selfish decision would bring me.

I fought the urge to fuck them both up and quickly spun on my heel and left without confrontation, refusing to believe the lies spewing from his black ass mouth. His betrayal sliced me deep. I'd chosen to see the best in Amir and to believe in the love we'd built. But my trust in him and in the concept of love as a whole crumbled.

Outside, the night air dried my tear-stained face. I walked toward my car, not knowing where in the hell to go. My mind replayed the scene repeatedly like a broken record—from the surprise visit I'd planned to the love I *thought* we had. All the good in my life felt like a foolish fantasy as I was swallowed up by my heartbreak over a love that was never meant to have a happy ending.

A COUPLE OF HOURS LATER, I'D TRANSFORMED MY HIGH-RISE Manhattan hotel room into a temporary salon with all the necessary tools for my wig install appointment. The New York skyline peeked through the heavy velvet curtains as I ambled over to let in Carissa, a first-time client who found me through my business Instagram page. I wasn't on social media as a person but a brand—never showing my face, only my work.

"Welcome, Carissa! I'm glad you could make it! Tell me about the occasion for your custom wig install."

"Thank you! I'm in my cousin's wedding this weekend, so you know I gotta slay."

"A wedding? That's exciting! Don't worry, girl. I'll make sure your wig is flawless. Do you have a particular style in mind?"

She shook her head. "Not really. I was thinking something elegant, but not too much like I'm going to prom or something. I saw your work online, so I trust your expertise."

I cracked a smile. "Bet. The good thing about wigs is they're versatile and easy to switch up your look without the long-term commitment of a cut or color change."

"Exactly! And with my busy schedule at the hospital, I need something as low maintenance as possible."

"I feel that. What do you think about long, soft waves for the wig? That way, you can pull it over to one side." I suggested while putting the drape around her to protect her clothes.

A grin sprang across Carissa's face. "I love that idea! It sounds perfect for the wedding."

She took a seat as I laid out my tools—combs, bonding glue, flat iron, and the star of the show, the handcrafted thirty-inch Brazilian body wave wig. My skilled fingers quickly braided down her freshly washed and blow-dried hair to create a flat base. Our conversation flowed effortlessly. We chatted about everyday life, what to do around her city, and everything in between.

"So, are you excited about being in your cousin's wedding?" I queried.

"Girl, it's shaping up to be the event of the season. But let me tell you, the drama behind the scenes could rival even the best soap opera."

"Really? Spill the tea."

"Well, the bride's ex showed up at her bridal shower last week begging for forgiveness for cheating on her with his ex. But not only did he cheat, he had the nerve to hit it raw and then came back to my cousin with a side baby begging like Usher in *Confessions*. Can you believe that shit? It was a hot ass mess!"

"That's bold as hell. What did your cousin do?"

"Oh, she called her brothers, and they got his ass up out of there real quick. Turns out his ass had the baby in the car outside and everything! It's so ghetto I can't stand it. But at least she said she's happy with her fiancé, even if her stalking ass ex keeps sending flowers and texting her and shit. It's seriously like a Tubi movie."

"Damn. That's some determination right there."

"And don't get me started on one of the other bridesmaids '*accidentally*' dying her hair purple, which will clash dramatically with our hot pink dresses. I swear she's gonna show up looking like the Cheshire Cat or Abby Cadabby or something. Now she's scrambling to fix it before the wedding. I should've told her to book an appointment with you!"

"Purple? Yikes! That's a nightmare. I'm only in town for the night, so good luck to her. I hope she sorts it out. Tell her to hit up somebody's beauty supply store."

Carissa chuckled. "And get this, my cousin told me earlier today that the groom's mother is trying to wear white! Of all colors! Every black woman knows the one color you're not supposed to wear to a wedding is white! There's a battle over that happening as we speak."

"Oh, hell no! I'm sure your cousin isn't having that."

"Absolutely not. But the juiciest tea is that the wedding planner is the best man's sneaky link, and she already got a man!"

My eyes widened. "Now that's some piping hot tea! Weddings really do bring out the dramatic flairs in people, don't they?"

"Right! I was saying the same thing to my mama the other day! Weddings and funerals are when all the skeletons come falling out of the closet. But despite all the mayhem, I think it will be a beautiful day, although it is calling for rain... and the wedding is outside."

As I continued working on Carissa's mane, we shared laughs and disbelief over her cousin's wedding shenanigans. Moments like those made me realize how much I loved my job. I aligned and secured the wig before styling it, snipping, and shaping it to frame Carissa's heart-shaped face and curling it. I aimed to make it look like it was growing from her scalp. Once complete, I held up the mirror to Carissa so she could see the finished product. Her smiling reflection beamed back at me.

"Oh my God! Thank you! It looks amazing! I feel like a brand new woman!"

My smile bubbled with satisfaction. "You're so welcome!"

———

AFTER A LONG SHOWER, I WAS READY TO RETREAT TO THE sanctuary of my hotel bed. I ordered room service for dinner with a glass of white wine and settled underneath the covers while looking for a movie to watch alone. I wrapped the comforter tighter around myself. The soft, white fabric was a poor substitute for the warmth of companionship, no matter how high the thread count. I looked around at the empty room, feeling the weight of my solitude as my eyes lingered on the vacant side of the king bed.

My mind wandered as *Love Don't Cost a Thing* played, and I ate my dinner in solitude. I felt like I was on a deserted island surrounded by a sea of people and still had no one to talk to. I turned off the TV, and the screen went black. I crawled out of bed and sailed over to the window, gazing at the city. A million lights flickered, drowning out competition from the stars. In silence, I allowed myself to feel the full extent of how lonely I was. Yeah, I got to travel and made good money doing hair, but the money couldn't keep me warm at night. It couldn't hold a conversation with me, and it damn sure couldn't fuck me.

"I need people," I mumbled to myself.

I decided to create a separate online presence from my hair business and reconnect with old friends. Maybe I'd even open my heart again to new possibilities. Whatever it was, I had to do something.

Amir

My bones settled into the plush leather seat of the first-class cabin. I was returning from Houston to Las Vegas, a trip I'd made more times than I could count. As I closed my eyes, a familiar scent wafted past my nose, a mix of sweet shea, rich vanilla, and golden honey I hadn't encountered in years.

I opened my eyes, and there she was—my ex-girlfriend, Nerissa, pushing the drink tray down the aisle with the grace of an angel. Rizzy was a vision, just like I remembered, looking like a melanated love letter from God himself. Her long, dark hair was perfectly styled in a high, sleek ponytail that stopped mid-back, and her mocha brown eyes glittered under the fluorescent lighting. Her crisp flight attendant uniform accentuated her slender but curvy figure and complemented her flawless caramel skin.

For a second, I was a statue, stunned by the sight of her aura after so long. The memories flooded back: the good, the bad, and the ugly. It was a part of my past I had tucked away, but it was in the flesh, live and in color, and moving closer with each click of her heels. My heart stumbled out a frantic beat as she approached. For a second, I wondered if she would even recognize me, and if she did, would she ignore me or stop and talk. The uncertainty of it all had my stomach knotted. I cleared my throat and waited for her eyes to meet mine. When they did, everything around me blurred. For a split second, there was no Vegas, no Houston, only her and me, suspended at a high ass altitude.

The tension between us was like a brewing volcano, seconds from erupting. My eyes popped wide with a mix of shock and a flash of affection that had never left my heart for her, while hers held a cautious balance of shock and professional control. Our eyes danced, having a wordless conversation. *I wonder what she's thinking. Should I apologize for what happened between us back then? Will an apology bridge the time gap after so long?*

She finally spoke my name. "Amir."

It was the origin of a conversation years in the making, a chance encounter at forty thousand feet that neither of us could have ever predicted in our wildest dreams. But there we were. I realized our love story hadn't ended. It had only been paused mid-sentence, waiting to be finished.

My voice was a low murmur as she paused by my seat. "Rizzy, it's been a minute," I acknowledged, my words hanging between us.

"It has."

"H-how are you? Are you... doing all right?" I questioned, the undertone of my concern for her safety evident.

"I'm good, Amir," Nerissa affirmed, though her glance away hinted that maybe our connection was something that not even Father Time could erase. She cleared her throat, regaining her professionalism. "Do you need anything? Can I get you something to drink?" she asked, glancing at her beverage cart.

I paused, making sure each word I spoke was carefully choreographed to avoid throwing salt in any old wounds. "Nah. I'm good for now. Thank you, though."

"Okay then."

She was about to proceed with her duties when the plane suddenly shook, rattling the overhead compartments and the glassware on her cart. The surrounding passengers gripped their armrests while others closed their eyes and prayed. The seat belt sign dinged above me as I watched Nerissa steady the cart and remind everyone to stay seated with skilled ease. Her demeanor remained professional despite the unsteadiness of the plane. I kept my eyes stationed on her, my heart racing, not from the bumpy flight but from the vicinity of her presence.

The turbulence passed, and the plane stabilized, but not before sending a stack of drink napkins on her tray fluttering to the ground. In a fleeting moment, we both reached for the same fallen napkin that had dropped between us. Our hands brushed a brief touch that sent a spark through me. It was accidental, but it felt like it meant something. My fingers grazed hers, feeling her hand tremble slightly. Up close, she smelled like a warm, comforting hug. *Damn. I wanna touch her but I know better.*

There were so many unspoken questions swirling in the silence between us. As we withdrew our hands, the space between us felt like miles. From the look in her eyes, there was an unspoken acknowledgment of the pain I'd caused her.

"S-So are you seeing anyone?" I quizzed, my deep voice barely above the hum of the plane's engines.

Before she could answer, the plane swayed violently. The sudden and severe turbulence had taken hold of the aircraft once again. The overhead lights flickered, and my ears pricked a unanimous gasp among passengers. Soon after, the captain's voice came in over the intercom.

"Ladies and gentlemen, this is your captain speaking. We've encountered an unexpected storm, and for your safety, we'll be grounding the plane to make an emergency landing in Phoenix. Please remain calm and follow the instructions of our skilled flight crew. As always, thank you for flying our airlines."

Nerissa's brown eyes ballooned before she straightened her posture and went into go mode, ensuring everyone in the cabin was buckled in and secure. She was the epitome of calm in the face of a storm. I wanted to hear her answer to my question to see if she'd found someone to fill the void after the damage I inflicted, but the severity of the moment had stolen my opportunity.

After the captain announced the emergency landing, I remained seated as everyone prepared to land. I reached into my pocket to pull out my phone. With a seasoned swipe, I unlocked the screen, the glow illuminating my face in the dimly lit cabin. I took the phone off airplane mode as my thumb hovered over the familiar green icon for my texts. I tapped it, and the list of messages appeared. There was nothing new from Brandi. The realization was both a relief and a disappointment. I didn't know what I expected after we had another blowup before I left for the airport. In my eyes, we were over. I locked the phone and slipped it back into my pocket as a light sigh escaped my lips.

The emergency landing in Phoenix was smooth despite the raging storm. Though irritating, the delay opened a portal to my past, and I was curious as hell about what lay on the other side, especially after seeing Nerissa after so long. Beneath my layer of irritation, I was grateful the storm had given us an unexpected overnight layover in the same city.

I couldn't help but wonder if the universe gave us a second chance to explore the 'what-ifs' that had come to the forefront of my mind after our initial encounter. I wondered if I'd get another opportunity to speak with her, to pick up our conversation where we left off, or if what we shared in the turbulent skies was all I'd be afforded. After all, seeing her again was a golden opportunity I hadn't expected.

Nerissa

I ushered a few steps into the dimly lit hotel bar, dressed in a stylish yet comfortable outfit—black high-waisted leggings, a scoop-neck white shirt, black leather jacket, and UGG Tasman Slippers. I felt the pleasant buzz of a few drinks I'd had a few hours earlier with my flight buddies at the airport after the storm and news of our unexpected layover in Phoenix.

I spotted an empty seat at the bar where a mix of hotel guests and locals were enjoying their drinks after a long day of work. I made my way over, ordering a top-shelf margarita. As I sipped my fourth drink of the night, I felt a light tap on my shoulder. Turning around, my eyes slightly widened, and my eyebrows heightened in surprise. I was shocked to see Amir standing there. Every muscle in my body momentarily tensed before I regained my composure. Seeing him again brought back a flood of memories that I wasn't prepared to deal with. Flashbacks of the fun times we shared and our undeniable connection replayed in my mind. He still had that rugged bad boy charm seeping through his pores. He was dressed casually and looked determined as hell to talk to me.

"Amir? I didn't expect to see you here," I said, although I was not surprised the airline had put him up at the hotel closest to the airport like everyone else.

"Mind if I join you for a drink?"

I hesitated for a moment but then nodded. "Sure, why not?" I replied, my tone friendlier than anticipated.

I briefly studied his profile as he took his seat beside me. He looked more mature for some reason. Granted, flexing in first class helped signify his grown-man status, but there was something more seasoned about his look that left a wet spot in my panties. Maybe it was the full beard that stretched across his face and perfectly connected to the mustache around the perimeter of his full lips. It suited him, amplifying his sex appeal in my eyes. A few more lines were etched across his handsome caramel features, making it clear his life hadn't been no crystal stair since we'd broken up. His demeanor seemed more composed, which made me wonder if he'd learned from his past mistakes or if he was putting up a good front.

He signaled the bartender for a drink, and my spine stiffened. We sat silently for a moment, the tension thick with unspoken words. I watched him order a classic Henny and Coke, sitting in silence as the bartender expertly mixed the drink, combining cognac, a couple of ice cubes, a few squirts of Coke, and an orange wedge for a garnish.

"So," Amir began after sipping from his drink, "I never got an answer to my question earlier."

"What question was that?"

"Are you seeing anyone?"

I paused, taking a sip of my margarita to gather my thoughts. As desperately as I wanted to come up with a witty comeback, the liquor in my system had me grasping at straws. I looked at Amir, noticing the sparkle of mischief still lingering in his eyes.

"Two and a half years go by, and that's the first thing you ask me?" I responded.

"I'm sorry. It's just seeing you again after so long, there's a lot of shit I wanna get off my chest."

I sighed. A part of me was relieved to know the elephant in the room hadn't gone unnoticed on his end, either. "Shoot."

"Look, I know this might not be the best time, but I want to apologize for how shit went down between us. I was immature and didn't handle things well. I've regretted it every day since."

Hearing Amir bring up the past made my body language shift. How could something feel like a lifetime ago and still feel like it happened yesterday? I set my glass down with more force than intended as my fingers tightened around the stem.

"You think an apology fixes everything? Do you know how bad you hurt me?"

His jaw clenched slightly as he looked down, feeling the weight of my response. "I know it doesn't, but I'll spend the rest of my life telling you how truly sorry I am for how I treated you."

I took a deep breath, my emotions swirling like a carousel. "Listen, Amir, I appreciate you saying that, but I'm not interested in reliving the past."

"So I guess it's pointless to ask if you ever think about us...? About me?"

My shoulders were relaxed but not fully leaning into the conversation as if I were interested. My arms rested on the bar, one hand occasionally playing with the stem of my margarita glass. "What did I just say, Amir?"

He nodded while his eyes searched mine for a sign of what I was truly feeling. "My bad."

"We can't change the past."

"But we can learn from it, right?"

"Is that what you did, Amir? Learned?"

"Hell yeah. I know I fucked up, and I've had years to think about it. When I saw you again, I knew I needed to make things right with you. Even if you never forgive me, I needed you to know how sorry I am. I just... I wish I handled your heart differently when I had the chance."

I gave him a onceover. There was a glint of sadness in his brown orbs, likely from his regrets, and a sincerity in his tone that hadn't been there previously. He seemed genuinely remorseful and eager to ensure I knew how sorry he was. The egotism that had sometimes colored his negative actions in the past had vanished, and in its place was humbleness.

I swallowed hard, teetering on the cliff of my rampant emotions. Despite Amir's apparent changes, the hurt from catching him cheating still lingered. Sure enough, all the anger I felt that night resurfaced, reminding me of the agony his whorish actions had caused. Yet, there was a nagging whisper inside me that remembered all the good times we shared and the connection we once had. While the idea of rekindling our past had crossed my mind, I'd never let him know that. Besides, I knew it would take a lot more than words to rebuild the trust and bond we used to have, no matter how fucking good he looked.

"To answer your original question, no. I'm not seeing anyone right now. I've been focusing on my career."

"You enjoy living out of a suitcase?"

I dipped my chin as I sat up straighter, eyes softening slightly. "Yeah. I do."

My tone was firm, and I maintained eye contact.

Amir looked more relaxed, a small smile playing on his lips as he offered an understanding nod. "That's wassup. I'm happy for you."

"Thanks. How's life been treating you over the years?" I inquired.

Of all people, I couldn't believe I was being nice to Amir. It was certainly nicer than I thought I'd be, asking about his current life and all when I knew damn well I didn't want to know about whoever he was fucking on. I decided to split the blame between the alcohol in my system and the nostalgia of old times.

Amir took a sip of his drink before shrugging his shoulders. "I could complain, but I won't... especially not after seeing you again."

"Two and a half years is a pretty long time."

A bittersweet expression masked his handsome face. "I'm glad we ran into each other, even if it's just for the night. Maybe this could be our chance to start over, even if it's just as friends."

I took a deep breath as my fingers danced across the sugared rim of my glass. "I already told you I don't want to rehash the past, and I damn sure don't want to be your friend, Amir."

He nodded slowly, his expression serious and respectful. His hands were still, resting on the bar. "Then what do you want, Rizzy?"

I looked down at his dick with a glimmer of seduction in my eyes. No other words were spoken. He finished his drink before standing up slowly and offering me the kind of devious smirk that told me I was in over my head. His movements were calm and deliberate, showing that he was with my decision and was ready to move forward with whatever the rest of the night had in store for us. The initial awkwardness between us melted away somewhere between the elevator and his hotel room. I had a hundred million reasons why I should've walked away, but none mattered when it came to Amir Patton. They never did.

With every minced step I took, it became harder for me to turn back, to wave my white flag and bow out, to change my fucking mind. My brain was either empty or had somehow been reprogrammed to only think about Amir and fucking. We weren't soulmates. Our meeting wasn't some sort of divine intervention from the fucking universe. And the things I was about to allow him to do to my body were most undoubtedly not left up to chance. Gone was the poor little brokenhearted girl still waiting for her happily ever after. I wanted to fuck.

The minute the door closed behind us, he kissed me. It wasn't an ordinary kiss. It was a kiss that harnessed all the unspoken feelings he could muster, making up for all the time our souls had spent trying to find their way back to each other. It sobered me up quick. His fingertips gently brushed against my cheek. It was soft and innocent but felt like everything I'd been missing. Under the shackle of his gaze, I felt beautiful.

His hands explored my body. "You're so fuckin' beautiful. Your body could get a nigga killed."

I pushed him back and took off my shirt as he sat on the edge of the bed, watching me come out of my clothes until I was completely naked. I stood bare, braving his gaze as I revealed my body to him. Our eyes maintained a flawless connection as he reached out his hand, drawing me to him. Something happened when a woman turned her heart loose to a bad boy. There was this sort of insanity behind knowing they'd ruin you in all the best fucking ways and going along for the ride anyway.

When I felt his hands against my bare skin, I flinched. I hadn't been touched with such a familiar gentleness in years. His touch, I would know it blind.

His tattooed hand inched down to cup my pussy. "Mmm, shit. She missed me as much as I missed her, huh?"

His baritone voice hit my ear, twisting up my insides. It arched my spine and made me bite my lip. The amount of inappropriate thoughts I had was alarming.

I panted. "I don't think I should be feeling like this."

"Like what?" he queried, his voice a husky whisper.

The hairs on my arms rose. "Like once I start, I'm not sure I'll ever want to stop."

Amir took my words for what they were: a challenge. He grabbed me by the throat but didn't choke me. Instead, he kissed me so profoundly that I swore my feet left the ground. Goosebumps swarmed every inch of my body. It was evident there was a raging fire between us that couldn't be doused.

"I missed the taste of your lips on mine," he whispered against my mouth.

With my eyes closed, I slowly dragged my fingers over his muscles. I still remembered the feeling of him under my palms, every curve of his biceps, the feel of every raised tattoo on his bronzed skin. Beneath the hurt and rage, I'd missed him, too—more than I realized. Amir's hands touched my sweet spot as if I was everything he'd ever prayed for, as if he'd gotten on his hands and knees and asked God to hand-deliver me himself.

"I love the way your breathing changes whenever I touch that pussy. It's been so long since I heard you moan my name."

He lowered himself between my thighs, sucking on my clit as I used his broad shoulders as leg rests.

I purred as I arched my back. "Mmmm, shit."

Amir pushed my legs up toward my chest and continued flicking his tongue against my softly waxed folds. I bucked forward as he inserted a finger inside me and finger fucked me too.

"Oh my God, Amir!"

"Say it again."

I moaned. "Fuck, Amir. It feels so fucking good."

Amir ate my pussy so good I couldn't control my moans, body movements, or thoughts. There were no words to describe how good it felt. If I had a thousand tongues, I still couldn't tell it all. The more he licked and slurped me up, the closer I got to super-soaking his beard.

"Oooh fuck! Fuck! Fuck! I'm about t-to c-cum!" I squealed, feeling all my muscles relax at once as I left a piece of my soul on his lips.

Before I could fully catch my next breath, he loosened his belt buckle and pulled his jeans and boxer briefs down to his ankles. I watched all nine inches of his brick-hard dick stand at attention. Every brown inch looked ready and willing to bust my pussy wide open. Amir had always had a fat dick, but it was thicker than I remembered. I bit down on my lip, eager to suck the nut out of his mushroom tip. I leaned forward, and he pulled my hair away from my face as I teased the head with my tongue.

"Mmm, shit." He growled.

He thrust his hips forward as I slobbed on the first few inches while jerking him off at the base.

I felt his dick pulse before he pulled away. "Fuck! Bring your sexy ass here."

Amir pushed me back onto the bed and pulled his shirt over his head, revealing a sea of tattoos covering his arms and chest. He climbed on top of me. His thick, gold Cuban link chain hung in my face as I traced his jawline while staring into his eyes. Amir's brown orbs were like pools of honey I could get lost in if not careful.

He kissed me slowly while running his fingers through my hair. Our foreheads touched as he pushed inside me. I gasped in his ear on the first thrust, and he held me close.

A soft moan slipped past my lips as he filled up my tight pussy inch by inch. "Oh my God."

Amir wore my smooth brown legs like a designer belt around his waist as he bucked his hips forward with deep strokes.

"Mmm, shit. I missed you, Rizzy. Fuckin' kiss me," he groaned while looking into my eyes.

I kissed him, our tongues swirling and exploring the depths of each other's mouths while breathing heavily. He picked up the pace while pushing my legs to his shoulders and holding onto my ankles. I squealed, feeling the curve of his dick hit my sweet spot with every stroke. He was driving me to my breaking point.

"Oh my God! Don't stop! Please don't stop! I'm about to cum again!"

"Look me in the eyes when you cum, Rizzy."

I opened my eyes and favored him with a euphoric stare. "I-I."

He gripped me by the throat. "Huh? I can't hear you."

"I-I'm c-cummmminnnggggg!"

Switching positions, he flipped me over on top of him. He gripped my ass cheeks, nails digging into my juicy flesh as I arched my back and eased down on top of him.

I tossed my head back, feeling my curls sweep the crack of my ass. "Oooh shit."

The liquor in my system had me throwing my ass in a circle while I bounced up and down. I mashed my palms into his chest, bucking harder and faster than I ever had before.

He smacked my ass as I leaned forward. My mouth was gaped open, only a breath away from his. "That's it! Ride that fuckin' dick."

I swatted my hair from one side of my face to the other, leaning to the side and looking back as he thrust upward into me. He gripped my throat before locking both hands behind my back and fucking my brains out.

I screamed. "Ooh fuck! Yes! Yes!"

I got up and turned around to ride him in the reverse cowgirl position. He gripped my waist from behind, fucking me without mercy. I leaned back against him so my spine was parallel to his chest. He slipped his hand over mine, hovering between my thighs as I stroked my throbbing clit. My body jerked hard, my legs shaking. He didn't care. He wasn't finished.

Amir smirked. "If you can still walk, we're not finished."

He peppered slow kisses on my smooth inner thighs before flipping me on top of him. "Ride my fuckin' face until you cum."

His long, warm tongue found my clit for the second time as I gripped the top of his head.

His firm hand smacked my ass so hard I knew he'd left a handprint behind. Still, I bucked like a prized racehorse as his tongue wrote love poems inside my folds.

"Holy shit! Don't stop, Amir. I'm so close!"

I rode him slowly, rotating my hips against his soft, full lips until my body shook with pleasure. After I came, he flipped me back onto my back and sucked on my diamond-hard nipples. He looked me in the eyes while his tongue licked over my mounds while rubbing my pussy. I *never* wanted the pleasure to stop. He was my darkest desire. I was his escape. And somewhere between the jagged edges of our fractured hearts was our deliverance.

Soon after, he snaked his dick inside me from the side, fucking me for a few strokes before flipping my legs over and fucking me missionary again. With each stroke, he had me begging and pleading for more.

We changed positions again. He forcefully bent me over, pressing my head into the crisp, white sheets so that I was face down, ass up. His dick drilled into me from behind, knocking my walls loose. I gripped the sheets, unable to run or tap out. All I could do was hold on for the ride. I looked back at him, my mouth gaped into an O shape as he leaned forward and grabbed my chin.

"You're so mothafuckin beautiful," he groaned as he pushed his thumb inside my mouth.

I sucked it like a lollipop before he pulled it out and yanked my hair so that I was forced to look up at the ceiling. All I heard between moans was the smacking of his thighs against my ass until he came.

Amir groaned. "Ahh, shit."

Amir

I stretched my tired limbs, reaching out to the other side of the bed, only to find it cold and vacant. My lashes shot upward, and my heart dropped half a foot when I realized Nerissa was gone.

"Rizzy?" I called out as I sat up while rubbing my eyes.

I looked around the room before climbing out of bed and checking the bathroom. All her things were gone, and she hadn't left a note or message. I instinctively checked my phone, hoping for a text, but there was nothing. I tried searching for her on social media again, but nothing came up. It was as if she'd vanished entirely.

I drew in a deep breath, feeling disappointment and acceptance. Nerissa's decision to have a drama-free departure after our night together felt like a sign from the universe. My thoughts transferred to Brandi back in Vegas as I stepped into the shower. Our relationship, or lack thereof, had been extremely volatile, but that didn't mean I didn't still love her. Nerissa's disappearance had unknowingly given me all the clarity I needed. Maybe it was time for me to focus on the present and fix things with Brandi.

After I showered and got dressed, I took the shuttle to the airport.

On the flight back to Vegas, I made a vow to myself that I'd put in the effort to improve things between Brandi and me. I knew it wouldn't be easy, but if she was going to be my wife, I had to put in the work. Forever was a very long time.

AFTER THE PLANE TOUCHED DOWN, I GRABBED MY CARRY-ON and shopped for Brandi's makeup gift at the Shops at Crystals. Walking into the Patek Boutique, I was greeted by the sparkle of diamond-encrusted, platinum, and gold watches. I browsed through the displays, looking for something that would surely split her face with a smile. After a few minutes, I spotted a beautiful watch with baguette-cut diamonds and blue sapphires. Blue was her favorite color. It felt perfect.

I stepped out of the store smiling when my eyes landed on Brandi's friend, Tasha. As soon as we made eye contact, I knew she would run her mouth to Brandi and let her know I was back in town. *Fuck.*

"Amir? What are you doing here?" Tasha quizzed, her eyes widening as she glanced at the bag in my hand.

"Sup, Tasha. Just picking up something special for B. I'm trying to make things right between us."

I had to set the record straight before she had Brandi thinking I was out there spending all my ends on some other woman.

Tasha nodded as a knowing smirk spread across her face. "Well, I'm sure she'll love it. I'll let my bestie know you're thinking about her."

I scoffed. "Yeah. I'm sure you will. You be easy, all right?"

She'd confirmed that Brandi would likely hear about the gift before I made it home. Maybe her blabbermouth friend would help show her how serious I was about repairing our relationship. With the gift, I headed home, ready to face whatever came next. I knew actions always spoke louder than words, and I was determined to show Brandi I was committed to taking our relationship to the next level. The only question was if she was as committed as me.

I STOOD OUTSIDE THE APARTMENT, MY HEART JACKHAMMERING in my chest. I drew in a deep breath, clutching the red gift bag. After a moment of hesitation, I inserted my key into the lock and turned the knob. My eyes landed on her in the living room. She was dressed in a strapless denim top and matching skort, taking a million different selfies of herself on the couch.

The expression on Brandi's face was a mix of surprise and curiosity when she saw me. "Amir? What are you doing here?"

"Hey, baby," I replied softly as my eyes met hers. "Can we talk?"

The atmosphere around us was tense as I sat on the couch. Brandi sat across from me, waiting for me to speak. "Go ahead."

"I know things have been rough as hell between us lately, but I want you to know that I love you, and I'm committed to making this shit work between us. I got you something to show how much you mean to me."

I handed her the Patek gift bag, and Brandi's eyes widened in surprise. She opened it slowly, revealing the brand-new sparkling watch. Her eyes filled with tears as she looked up at me.

"Aww, baby, it's beautiful," she whispered through a cheesy grin. "You didn't have to do this. I mean, you did, but you didn't."

"You my baby, and you're about to be my wife. I wanted to," I replied, reaching out to take her hand. "I'm serious about us, B. I know I've made mistakes, but I'm ready to put in the effort to make things right if you are."

Brandi looked at the sparkling watch that matched her outfit perfectly, then back at me. She nodded slowly as she sprung a grin on her soft lips.

"Thank you, baby," she said, her voice filled with emotion. "I appreciate this bomb-ass watch and you for finally putting me first and showing me you're all in. I forgive you and want to work on this together too."

"So this means you're gonna put your ring back on now?"

She grinned. "Yes."

A wave of relief washed over me. I hugged Brandi gently, holding her body close to mine. At that moment, flashes of the night before with Nerissa flooded my brain. I felt a twisted mix of emotions about having her and what happened between us in the back of my mind. On the one hand, I felt a slight sense of closure, knowing that her abrupt departure was a sign to focus on what I had going on with Brandi. On the other, there was also a lingering sense of unresolved feelings and what-ifs that I couldn't shake.

Brandi brought my thoughts back to the present when she pushed me back onto the couch and dropped between my legs. She unbuckled my jeans and unzipped them before I eased up to pull them down to my ankles.

"I'm tired of fighting, baby. Aren't you?"

Before I could give her an answer, she spat on her palms and started rubbing my dick, lathering it with her saliva.

I grunted. "Shit. Yeah. I am."

She smirked. "Good."

Brandi leaned forward, licking from the base of my dick to the tip while never breaking eye contact with me. *Mmm, fuck. She knows I like that freaky shit.* She ran her smooth hands up and down the base while sucking on the head. I pulled my shirt over my head before reaching forward to pull down her top, eager to see her perky caramel tits. I pushed her dark hair out of her face, never wanting to miss a second of how good she looked with my dick in her mouth.

"Oh *fuck.*"

Brandi's long tongue flicked the tip of my dick before she deep throated me. She twisted her neck like *The Exorcist*, gagging on my dick with her hands behind her back. My toes curled in my shoes. Her head game was top-tier and had me ready to sing out *throat babyyyyyy.* She came up for air after sucking the soul out of my meat with spit shining around her lips. My dick was bathed in her saliva as she jacked me off with both hands. Her full lips were covered in a sheen of glossy spit. I felt myself succumbing to the pleasure as she sucked and massaged my balls while jerking me off. Brandi had me ready to turn her throat into a daycare. *Fuck.*

I licked the palm of my hand before rubbing my shaft. "Bend that fuckin' ass over," I demanded.

I smacked her ass, and she did as she was told. I eagerly slapped the tip of my dick against the crack of her ass before sliding inside. *What the fuck was I even mad for again?*

Nerissa

I sat by my apartment window, lost in thought, the soft hum of the city outside barely registering. A week had passed since I'd let Amir inside me again for the first time in two and a half years. The memory of that night in the hotel room came flooding back, uninvited and stubbornly refusing to leave my mind.

I had watched him sleep, his handsome brown face at peace, an evident difference from the turbulence inside my heart. We'd reconnected by chance on that plane and again that night at the bar. It felt like destiny. But the longer I stared at the rise and fall of his bare chest, the old wounds began to fester, and all my pent-up resentment bubbled to the surface. Lying next to him, feeling our bodies touch again after so long, I felt suffocated by the weight of our connection.

So, I decided to leave in the quiet morning hours before the sun rose. I eased out of bed and redressed silently, careful not to wake him. As I stood by the door, I hesitated. A foolish part of me screamed to stay, to give Amir a second chance. But fear of repeating the past had won me over. I slipped out of the room without a word, leaving only the night's memories and the scent of my perfume on his sheets.

After leaving, I couldn't shake the feeling of regret. I wondered if my leaving had ruined our last chance to start over. The thought gnawed at my insides, a constant reminder of what could have been. I sighed while running my hand through my hair. I knew dwelling on the past wouldn't help my future, but the regret lingered in the pit of my stomach.

THE NEXT DAY, MY THOUGHTS WERE STILL TANGLED WITH memories of Amir as I sat in the crew lounge awaiting our flight to Atlanta. My friend and fellow flight attendant, Jamia, plopped down beside me. Her comforting brown eyes swept over me. She had a knack for sensing when something was off.

"Hey, boo. Wassup with you?"

"Hey. I'm good."

"You sure? Because you look like you're carrying the weight of the world on your shoulders today," Jamia stated, her tone gentle but obviously probing.

I sighed, knowing I couldn't keep my feelings bottled up any longer. "It's my ex. I saw him again after a long time, and now I can't stop thinking about his ass. I think I may have ruined our last chance to make things right."

Jamia listened intently, her cocoa brown expression filled with empathy. "I get it. Breakups fucking suck, especially when there sounds like there's some unfinished business between you two. How long has it been since y'all ended things?"

"A couple of years."

She held her finger up, putting a pin in the conversation while she swept one of her boho braids behind her ear. "*Years?* Damn, girl. The D must be A-1 because why else would you be living in the past?"

I chuckled. "Shut up."

"Seriously, though. You're a great catch, and just because you may have missed your chance with your ex doesn't mean you have to miss out on giving yourself a chance to move forward."

I nodded, knowing Jamia was right, but I still felt a twinge of regret in my chest. "I guess I just don't know how to let shit go."

Jamia's teeth flashed white and broad as her eyes gleamed with mischief. "Well, we're landing in Atlanta tonight, right? How about we do something fun? Somebody told me there's a speed dating event for black singles downtown, like every Thursday at this lounge in Buckhead. It could be a great way to meet new people and at least give us a few laughs before we fly out in the morning. No harm, no foul, right?"

I hesitated at the idea of putting myself out there again. The feeling was both exciting and nauseating. "Speed dating? I don't know, Jamia..."

"Come on, it'll be fun! And who knows, you might meet Mr. Replacement. At the very least, it'll be a good distraction," she encouraged with a gentle nudge.

I drew in a deep breath before deciding to take the plunge. "Fuck it, let's do it. Maybe it's time I start looking forward instead of backward."

Jamia's red painted lips spread with a grin as she clapped her hands. "That's the spirit! Let's get ready to show Atlanta our worst tonight."

As we boarded the plane and prepared for our flight to Atlanta, I felt a tiny flicker of hope ignite inside my chest. Maybe it was the kick in the ass I needed to get out of my feelings.

***

THE SPEED DATING EVENT IN ATLANTA WAS HELD AT AN upscale lounge in Buckhead with dim lighting and a poppin' atmosphere. I wore my hair in a high, sleek ponytail with dangling hoop earrings and a military green strapless cargo pants jumpsuit with strappy gold heels. Jamia was clad in a mid-length jean jacket, black jean miniskirt, Balmain crop top, and booties with her boho braids pulled up into a cute half-up, half-down style.

Upon entrance, Jamia and I were greeted by a venue buzzing with excitement. The room was filled with melanin-rich people eager to connect with someone, if only for the night. Soft R&B music played in the background, adding to the relaxed yet sophisticated vibe. The friendly host handed us name tags and explained the rules. Each participant had five minutes to chat with a possible love match before the bell rang. When that happened, the men had to move on to the following table while the women remained seated. The goal was to meet as many people as possible and see if any connections could be forged.

My nerves were wracked as I sat at one of the candlelit cocktail tables. Jamia winked at me from her table across the room, subtly reminding me to have fun and stay relatively loose.

The first few rounds were a blur of introductions and meaningless conversations. I encountered a variety of men, each with unique looks and personalities. There was a handsome architect with a bald head and salt and pepper beard who loved to build, a nerdy software developer with a matted afro and an obsessive passion for gaming, and a witty college professor, who resembled Blair Underwood in his prime, who spent the entire five minutes blabbing about his love for science.

Yet, as the evening wore on, I found myself seated across from a handsome man named Micah. He had a fresh, trendy haircut, warm smile, and an easygoing vibe that immediately settled my bouncing nerves. We exchanged the initial banter that all strangers did before I discovered that he was attractive and genuinely interesting. Micah was a graphic designer who was originally from Dallas. He moved to Atlanta a few months prior after a bad breakup with his ex. I empathized with his need for a new start while laughing at his jokes, sharing stories about my job as a flight attendant, and even tossing a few flirtatious glances his way. In five minutes, he reminded me how good it felt to be out and about.

As the bell rang, signaling the end of our short time together, Micah leaned in slightly, his eyes determined. "I hope I'm not being too forward, but I really enjoyed talking with you. I feel like you're the best, if not the only, connection I've made all night. I know you don't stay around here, but maybe when you're back in the city, we could grab a coffee sometime and continue this conversation?"

Contentment hooked my mouth, feeling a warmth I hadn't felt in a while spread through me. "I'd like that," I replied before exchanging contact information with him.

Despite my enjoyable time and the romantic chemistry between Micah and me, I couldn't shake the feeling that something was still holding me back from entirely putting everything with Amir to rest. As much as I was feeling Micah's vibe, I knew deep down that I wasn't ready for anything serious, at least not with him. My heart was still healing, and I needed more time to move on entirely and shake Amir for good.

ANOTHER HOUR OR SO PASSED BEFORE JAMIA AND I LEFT THE event. I was grateful for the new experience and the chance to meet Micah, but I also knew I had to be upfront with myself about where I was emotionally.

"So... how was it? Give anybody your number?" Jamia probed, linking arms with me as we got into our Uber for a ride back to the hotel.

"It was great," I said, smiling at her. "I gave one guy my number."

"Which one?"

"Micah."

"The chef?"

"No. The graphic designer from Dallas."

"Hmm. I don't remember him."

"Yeah, well, he was cool. But I think I need to focus on myself for a bit longer before diving into anything new."

Jamia nodded with understanding. "That's fine. The important thing is that you put yourself out there and had a good time tonight. The right man will come along to sweep you off your feet when the time is right and not a second before."

I squeezed Jamia's arm. "Thanks, girl. I needed this."

"No problem, girl."

Amir

Ahsan, XL, and I stood at Big Mama's grave inside the quiet cemetery on a sunny afternoon. We paid our respects for her birthday with fresh flowers and kisses to her engraved jet-black headstone.

I knelt by the grave, placing my bouquet of violets by her name. "Big Mama always knew how to keep our asses in check. I hope I can do the same."

Ahsan placed a hand on my shoulder. "You will, nigga. You've got this. And remember, I'm right here if you need me."

"Any word from Jules or Sienna's ex?"

He grunted. "Not a fuckin' word from her since the text she sent. That nigga's been quiet too."

XL looked around before speaking. "There's something I need to show y'all."

"What is it?"

"I was looking over the security camera footage from the barbershop from last night, and I saw a shadowy figure dressed in all black lurking around near the back entrance. Someone I didn't recognize at first."

"Who the fuck was it?" Ahsan asked before I had the chance to.

"The figure stepped into the light for just a second, and I saw it was Jules."

My brother gritted his teeth. "I knew it. What the fuck was that bitch up to?"

"I went to the shop early this morning and found one of the books with information on our stash house locations was missing. I think she's got it."

"What the fuck? How the fuck did she even get in? We got all her tech and changed the locks months ago! She's never had access to your shop."

We all paused, standing in the deafening silence as our minds wandered. "Fuck." XL hissed.

"What? What is it?"

"You remember about six months back when we were out on that trip to Miami, and our returning flight got delayed?"

"What about it?"

"I had the delivery guy coming to my shop to drop off the supplies like he does every week, and nobody was there to let him in. And you—"

"I told you to call Jules and see if she could handle it," Ahsan interrupted, finishing his sentence.

"I told her where the spare key was. I thought she'd returned it, but maybe she made a copy of it and has had it all this time. When I got all her shit back and changed the locks at the office, I never changed the locks at the shop."

"Man, fuck!" Ahsan roared, losing his usually cool edge.

I surged upright, frowning and clenching my fists. "All right, XL. I need you to get the locks at the shop changed and we need to figure out how to retrieve that book. We can't afford any fucking leaks right now."

"Especially not with my land deal with the mayor," Ahsan griped. "I will not let that bitch fuck this up for me right when I have everything I want."

"Don't worry about it, nigga. We gon' handle it before it ever comes to that."

"Amir, like I said, I'm here if you need me, nigga. Just say the word," Ahsan repeated, itching to take over the wheel.

I took a deep breath. "Thanks, but I want you to keep your hands clean and enjoy the normalcy of your new legitimate ass life. You trusted me to handle it, and that's what I'm gonna do. These niggas know I'm new in the lead position. They're targeting me. But let them mothafuckas try. I'll be ready."

"Any word about Rico?" Ahsan asked.

I swung my head in a no. I'd been on the hunt for Rico as a personal favor to my brother ever since he and Bradley conspired to take my brother's life. Since I'd taken over the business for Ahsan, I'd put a hit out on Rico's head, spreading the word wide and far that if anyone informed me of his whereabouts, I'd pay them a hefty sum to bring him to me alive. I'd killed two niggas in two months looking for his ass around the city and still hadn't come up with shit.

"I don't like this shit," XL stated. "We got too many niggas gunning for us in different directions."

"I don't like it either." My brother agreed.

My eyes narrowed as a million thoughts sped through my mind. "XL, I need you to tighten security around your barbershop and the office until we figure out how to get that fuckin' book back."

"Let me sweep her apartment for it," Ahsan offered. "I don't care if I have to pry it from her cold, dead fingers."

"No. Let XL handle it. Ahsan, keep your ears open. Let me know immediately if you hear anything about Sienna's ex."

Ahsan dipped his chin. "All right. I got you. Just be careful, nigga."

I nodded. "I will."

After leaving Ahsan and XL, I sat in the car and tried accessing my social media accounts to make a remembrance post about Big Mama's birthday and noticed I was locked out of all my fucking accounts.

"What the fuck?" I mumbled. Initially, I thought it was some sort of random tech glitch, but after a few unsuccessful attempts, I knew something was off.

I sucked my teeth, getting more pissed off by the second. When I tried resetting the passwords, none of the recovery emails came through to my inbox. I was two seconds away from throwing my fucking phone out of the window when it hit me. *I know this bitch fuckin' didn't.*

My face screwed into a grimace. Brandi had changed everything. My frustration flourished as I pieced it all together, ready and willing to confront her childish ass.

I sped home and stormed into the apartment, my mind racing as I prepared to go to war with her ass. I found her lounging on the couch, scrolling through her phone as if nothing was wrong.

"What the fuck is good with your ass, B? Huh? You think this shit is fucking funny?" I confronted her with a sharp bark.

She glanced up, faking her innocence. "I don't know what you're talking about."

"Oh. You don't know what the fuck I'm talking about, huh? All right, bet." I held up my phone, showing her the screen with my locked social media account on display. "Why the fuck did you change all my fucking passwords, Brandi?"

She smirked, no longer bothering to hide her cynicism as she shrugged. "Because I felt like it. Got a problem with that?"

My anger brewed beneath my skin. "Are you fucking serious? The fuck kind of answer is that? You can't just take control of my accounts without fucking asking me!"

She rolled her eyes dramatically. "Oh, please, nigga. Your ass spends too much damn time on there looking at other bitches anyway. Consider it a fucking favor,"

I sucked my teeth. "You just running your mouth, not knowing what the fuck you are even talking about, per usual," I countered, my voice rising. "I'm a grown-ass man! You can't just invade my fuckin' privacy like that."

She shot to her feet and crossed her arms defiantly. "Maybe if your shady ass didn't have anything to hide, you wouldn't care so much. Why are you so pressed, Amir? Who the fuck you got waiting in your DMs, huh?"

I took a step back, being mindful to keep my distance. "This isn't about hiding anything. It's about fuckin' boundaries, Brandi. If we're going to make this shit work, your ass needs to respect me and my shit!"

She scoffed before turning away to storm down the hallway. "Whatever, nigga! Do whatever you want like you always do."

I sighed, feeling the situation's sourness and its effect on my mood. "I'm fucking serious, Brandi. If your ass can't respect my privacy, then fuck a wedding. We need to rethink this entire relationship!"

She didn't bother to respond. Instead, she slammed the bedroom door. As badly as I wanted her to shut the fuck up, her silence spoke volumes.

Nerissa

My phone buzzed with an incoming FaceTime call from Demario. I answered, smiling at the sight of his familiar face. It had been a few weeks since we'd linked up in Vegas, and we hadn't spoken since.

"Hey, sis! Wassup with you? How's it going?"

"Hey, Maree! I'm good. I just got back home after working a three-day shift. What's up?"

"Listen, I heard you that night when we met up. I know you wanted me to do something constructive with my life. So, I have this amazing business idea."

"Okay... what is it?" I asked with hesitance laced in my voice.

"I want to start a mobile car detailing service. It's going to be huge, sis. All I need from you is some initial funding, y'know, to get it off the ground."

I raised an eyebrow, skeptical. Although I was glad to hear a different plan than reverting back to the streets, I still wasn't sold. "What the hell is a mobile car detailing service, Maree? Have you done any research? Do you even have a business plan? Do you even have a personal bank account set up, let alone a business account?" I probed, sounding more like a mother than a sister.

He sucked his teeth. "See, I knew you were gonna ask all that. Yes, I've done my homework. I have a solid plan, and I know it can work. I just need a little help from you to get started."

I sighed, thinking about my financial responsibilities. "Exactly how much help are we talking about?"

"I only need fifteen hundred dollars to get everything set up."

I sighed. "And what do fifteen hundred bucks get you?"

"Everything I need. My license, my fees, everything."

I sighed, smelling the lie through the phone. "All right, Maree. Fine. I'll help you out just this once, but you better make that shit work. And the next time I'm in town, you better make my car sparkle."

He cheesed, looking like a younger version of our father, and my heart melted just a little bit. "Thank you, Rizzy! Forreal, yo. I swear on our dad's grave, I won't let you down this time!"

"Remember, this is a loan. I expect your ass to pay me back, even if it's in installments, once you start turning a profit."

"Oh, absolutely, Rizzy. I won't forget."

"Where do you want me to send you the money? Western Union? Zelle?"

"Nah. Send it to my girl's bank account."

I paused. "Your who?"

He angled the camera to the left, revealing a woman I'd never seen before, and said, "I want you to meet someone."

She cheesed and waved. She had an espresso-brown complexion, smooth skin, a pearly white smile, and expressive cocoa-brown eyes. Her frame was slender, and her hair was done in a fresh sew-in with a voluminous side part to the left.

"Hi, Nerissa! I'm Jules. It's so nice to meet you. Demario has told me so much about you."

I gridded my teeth into a polite smile, trying to mask my confusion and shock. "Nice to meet you too, Jules. That's a pretty name."

"Thank you."

"So, where did you two meet?" I quizzed.

"We met at a mutual friend's barbecue a few months ago. We felt a spark right away."

"And how long have you been dating? Because I saw my brother just a little over a month ago, and he never mentioned you. With a name as pretty as yours, I'd remember it."

"We've been together officially for about three weeks now. It's been fast but amazing. I can't speak for your brother, but I've enjoyed every second of this."

I nodded, still feeling protective of my brother, but he was a grown-ass man. Who was I to stand in his way of happiness or whatever the fuck they had going on. "Well, I'm glad to hear that. Take good care of him."

"I will."

"I want you two to meet the next time you're in Vegas."

I bobbed my head. "Yeah. Sure. That sounds good."

"So, listen, I'll text you her routing and account number so you can transfer the money, all right?"

I frowned. "Hold up, I don't feel right transferring that much money into a stranger's account. I know I was a little harsh before, but do you seriously not have a bank account set up?"

"Chill, it's not like that. Jules is a good girl. I trust her. Please, just do this for me. You said you would."

I drew in a deep breath before reluctantly agreeing to transfer the money. "Okay, fine. I'll do it."

"Hit me and let me know when it's done?"

"Yeah. Okay. I'll text you."

"Bet. Thank you again, sis. I owe you."

"You damn right you do."

"Bye." Jules waved, showing damn near all thirty-two of her white ass teeth.

"See ya," I replied before ending the call.

After the call ended, I sat back, lost in thought. Not only did something about Demario and his new girl seem off, but there was something about seeing my brother with someone of his own that made my mind drift to memories of Amir. I sighed, feeling a mix of emotions that sent a wave of nausea rolling through my stomach. I gasped.

Suddenly, I realized my period was a few days later than usual. I quickly scrolled through my calendar app to check the days. I was going on day six, and my period came like clockwork every twenty-eight days. No stops. No delays. *Fuck. Don't trip, Rizzy. Don't jump to conclusions. You've been stressed as hell lately, right? It's gotta just be that.* I scrolled to my reminder app to write a note to get a pregnancy test in another few days if it still hadn't come.

Amir

It was date night. The four of us—Ahsan, Sienna, Brandi, and I —were at a Michelin-starred restaurant known for its exquisite views of the Vegas Strip and five-star service. My brother and Sienna were almost sickening to be around. He couldn't keep his hands off her, and she had no plans of stopping him. PDA be damned. Brandi and I, on the other hand, were, once again, not on the same page.

The evening started off fine. We were seated at a prime table, enjoying the chef's tasting menu. The conversation between us flowed easily, filled with laughter. Brandi and Sienna showed off their rings and talked about wedding plans. The sommelier had just poured a new wine for us to try—some expensive, tart-ass red wine. Everything went to shit when the waitress, a cute woman with a friendly smile, brought the next course. All I fucking said was thank you.

Brandi cut her eyes at me. "Really, nigga?"

I frowned. "What?"

A raging storm brewed in her eyes. "You really gonna check out that bitch's ass like I'm not sitting right beside your stupid ass?" she accused, voice rising, drawing the attention of nearby diners.

I scoffed. "Yo, chill. All I fuckin' said was thank you."

"Don't tell me to fucking chill. I know what the fuck I saw! You were practically drooling over that ho!"

Across the table, Ahsan and Sienna exchanged glances.

"Yo, let's not make a scene," my brother said sternly.

But it was too fucking late. The other diners had noticed, and the room seemed uncomfortably silent. I felt the heat of embarrassment creeping up the back of my neck. I glanced around, seeing the curious and judgmental stares of strangers around us.

"Brandi, please," I pleaded, my voice barely above a whisper. "I wasn't doing shit."

Her eyes flashed with rage. "I can't believe you would disrespect me like this, fucking playing in my face in front of everyone. I knew I shouldn't have put this dumb ass ring back on so soon!"

My fist slammed against the table, rattling the silverware and spilling some crimson wine. "So take it the fuck off!" I boomed, losing my cool.

Our evening was ruined. My rage-filled gaze shot over to Ahsan and Sienna, and I noticed they seemed just as uncomfortable and unsure of what I'd do next as I did.

The waitress, sensing the tension, reapproached the table cautiously. "Is everything all right over here?" she asked. The unease in her voice was evident.

I tried to force a smile, but I didn't give a fuck about trying to salvage the situation. The damage was done. If Brandi wanted a battle, I'd give her ass war.

Sienna spoke up first. "Yes, everything's fine. Just a little misunderstanding."

"Since your dream girl is back, why don't you go on and get her number while she's here, Amir. Go on. Go ahead. Pull out your phone. At least have the decency to do it to my face rather than behind my back, you coward!"

The waitress stood at the head of the table, looking stunned and confused. "I'm sorry. I don't understand—"

"Excuse her," I interjected. "She ain't take her meds today. You good."

"Nigga, fuck you! You know I'm not on no fucking medication!"

"Well then, maybe you ought to be because this isn't the first time you've accused me of this shit, and I'm tired of it."

Ahsan and Sienna looked on before my brother tried to intervene. "Yo, y'all need to take this shit outside and cool off."

I waved him off before continuing, my voice firm. "Brandi, I'm forreal. I'm tired of this shit."

"And I'm tired of you."

"I told your ass I wasn't flirting, trying to get her number, or none of that. I was just being polite. It's called mothafuckin manners. That should be the end of it. Your insecurities are your problem, not mine! You need to trust me, and if you can't, you can leave the ring on the table and find your own way home." I barked, feeling the ten-ton weight of embarrassment and frustration.

I threw down my napkin and stormed out of the restaurant. Ahsan quickly followed me, leaving behind Sienna to try and calm Brandi's toxic ass down.

<hr>

OUTSIDE, THE DRY NIGHT AIR GREETED ME AS I PACED BACK AND forth, trying to stop myself from catching a case. Ahsan caught up to me and placed his hand on my shoulder. "Yo. You straight? Shake that shit off and take a deep breath. You don't want to do something you'll regret, nigga. She got you locked up once; don't think she won't do it twice."

I halted mid-step, my face a mix of anger and confusion as my chest deflated with a hard sigh. "I can't do this shit, Ahsan. I can't marry her. She brings out the fucking worst in me."

He nodded, understanding. "I've seen it firsthand. And I don't want you to make a mistake you can't come back from behind her. There's too much at stake. If you're not ready, you need to tell her."

I pushed out another hard sigh while running a hand over my beard. "Listen, you remember when I flew out to see Jefe a few weeks back? Then I stopped in Houston?"

"Yeah. What about it?"

"You remember my ex, Nerissa? The one I was with before I got with Brandi?"

"Barely. But what about her?"

"Well, I ran into her on the flight from Houston back home, but we ran into a storm and had to do an emergency landing in Phoenix. I'm not chicken tender, but seeing her again made me realize I'm still in love with her. I don't know if that's even possible, but it's how I feel. I don't want to hurt Brandi, but I know I can't marry her when my heart beats for someone else."

Ahsan looked at me with concern etched on his face. "You need to tell her the truth, nigga. It's not fair to either of you to go through with this if you're not fully committed. And after what I just witnessed, neither of you are."

I nodded slowly, the weight of the decision settling on my shoulders. "You're right. I'll talk to her. But not here, not after all this shit."

Ahsan gave me a supportive clap on the back. "You'll figure it out. Just don't rush into anything. Take the time you need to sort out your fucking feelings, nigga."

As we headed back inside, I knew what I needed to do, even if it would be difficult. The night may have taken a turn for the worse, but it also brought me a moment of truth I couldn't ignore. Brandi was a mothafuckin problem.

Nerissa

Four more days passed before I worked up the nerve to buy and take a pregnancy test. I stood in the airport bathroom, held up in the private stall, as the space around me bustled with travelers coming and going from point A to Z. Feeling trapped, I looked up. The fluorescent lights cast a cold, unflattering glow on the walls around me.

Dressed in my crisp uniform, my expression was masked with anxiety as I waited for the timer on my phone to sound off. I closed my eyes, counting the seconds. *Three. Two. One. BING.* My hands trembled slightly as I held the pregnancy test. I pulled a breath through my nostrils, trying to steady my heartbeat, before I looked at the results. The airport's noise faded into the background as I focused on the small plastic stick in my hand. When I finally looked, my heart dried up in my chest. The test showed two lines in the results window. *Positive.* I was pregnant. I was pregnant with Amir Patton's baby.

My mind immediately raced with a whirlwind of emotions—shock, fear, and a sudden twinge of excitement. As a protective gesture, I instinctively touched my flat belly, which would soon grow.

Trying to process the life-changing news was more challenging than I expected. I knew I needed to tell Amir about my discovery, but the thought of contacting him after leaving how I did in Phoenix did nothing but fill the pit of my stomach with dread.

***

LATER THAT EVENING, THE INSIDE OF MY HOTEL ROOM WAS dimly lit with the soft glow of my phone screen illuminating my face. After spending the past eight hours in the sky, I'd landed in Dallas for an overnight. I wore a comfortable matching Sherpa loungewear set while setting up my personal Facebook page. Somewhere among the clouds, I'd found the determination to find Amir online so I could share my news.

My narrow fingers hovered over the keyboard as I typed his name into the search bar. Within moments, I found his profile. My heart rattled inside me as I scrolled through his most recent posts. I stopped when a video from a few months back caught my eye. It turned out to be from his thirtieth birthday party. Seconds after hitting play, I watched him get down on one knee and propose to another woman.

The initial shock hit me like an elbow to the face, leaving me momentarily breathless. The sight triggered an unexpected flood of painful memories of his cheating ways. My heart chilled after watching him slide the ring on her finger. There was a pang in my chest with the realization that he'd somehow managed to find happiness with someone else. *How could he move on so quickly after what he did to me?* I exited the app, unable to stomach the thought of watching them kiss. Where did an unexpected baby fit into his plan to run off into the sunset with someone else?

I sat up and reopened the app to check the date. "Hold up. This nigga was engaged when he slept with me?" I blurted out, instantly realizing not a damn thing about him had changed.

Anger flowed through me, a burning sensation radiating from the center of my chest. *That nigga never deserved my love or a second chance to fuck me again!*

My mind replayed the sight of him down on one knee, smiling at another woman who wasn't even all that. It felt like a cruel twist of fate. The proposal video reminded me of the life I thought we would build together and the family I knew we'd never be.

Tears welled up in my eyes. "I can't keep letting this nigga's moves control my happiness," I muttered, swiping away my tears.

I thought back to the positive pregnancy test. Since an abortion wasn't a road I wanted to go down, I knew I had to focus on my well-being and my baby. If that meant keeping my distance from Amir to keep my stress levels down, then so be it. Fresh tears filled my eyes as the thought of going through pregnancy alone loomed over me, but I quickly wiped them away. For my sanity and the well-being of my unborn child, I needed to keep my distance from Amir and his endless female drama. I decided then and there to tell him about the baby after it was born. I couldn't handle him being so heavily involved in the pregnancy so early trying to control my life while I had no power over his.

"I have to protect my peace and my child."

I placed a hand on my stomach, feeling a sense of purpose toward the new life growing inside me. *This baby is my future now.* I knew the road ahead would be challenging, but I was ready to face it head-on for myself and my baby.

Amir

I knew something was wrong the minute my phone rang. I could feel it in the pit of my stomach right before I answered it. The moment I did, my mug immediately turned stern.

"What the fuck do you mean the product is gone? How the fuck could this happen right before the trucks are supposed to leave?"

"We don't know. Three of our stash houses were broken into last night. A lot of the product is missing," the muffled voice of one of my lieutenants replied.

I was frustrated beyond words. "Fuck! This is a goddamn disaster. Don't do anything until I get there. I'll be there in ten minutes," I said before hanging up and immediately calling Ahsan.

"Sup?" He answered after the third ring.

I sighed into the receiver. "We've been hit—three stash houses. A huge chunk of our product is gone. I need you to meet me ASAP."

"What? Three? Fuck! Okay. I'm doing a final walk-through with the inspector in ten minutes. I'll get up with you soon after. Hit XL and tell him what's up."

"Bet."

Two hours passed, and I was still visibly upset. I paced back and forth as the three of us reviewed the security camera footage. Multiple screens showed different camera angles. XL and Ahsan sat in front of the security monitors, focused, trying to piece together the puzzles. Ahsan rewound the footage to the previous night. We watched intently as figures dressed in hoodies moved swiftly through the houses, loading our product onto a truck and speeding off.

Ahsan pointed at the screen. "Hold the fuck up. That mothafucka right there! I think I recognize him."

I squinted. Maybe he looked familiar, but I couldn't place him quickly enough.

XL paused the footage. "Wait... I think I've seen that nigga before too. I've seen him hanging around Jules's apartment. You don't think..."

"Holy fuck. First, that bitch steals the book with our stash house locations, and now those same houses just so happen to get hit before our shipment was set to go out? That's too much of a coincidence for me," my brother stated.

XL nodded. "And it's not like she doesn't know the shipment schedule."

"Fuck!" I roared, ready to rip a mothafucka to shreds. "So she's working with him. We need to find out more about this nigga. Do you remember anything specific about him when you saw him around Jules?"

Ahsan sat quietly, eyes still glued to the screen as he leaned back in his chair, thinking hard. "Oh shit," he blurted out before XL could respond.

"What?"

"That's not just *any* nigga. That's Demario, Sienna's ex."

I frowned. "Her ex? Nigga, are you sure?"

"Yeah. I got a picture of him on my phone. She showed him to me after he threatened her in the grocery store a while back. I thought this nigga was laying low because he may have been working with the Feds or something, but now it's looking like he wants to take a piece of our empire for himself."

Ahsan pulled out his phone and showed us the photo. Lo and behold, it was him. I sighed. "So it's personal. You've got his girl, and now he's got our product."

"It's feeling that way," he replied. "Jules knows exactly what she's doing. I never should have trusted that bitch."

"Hold up. Let's dig into this shit for a minute," XL interjected. "Why would Jules get with Sienna's ex, of all people?"

"To get back at me for choosing Sienna over her. I don't know what makes a mothafucka crazy. I just know you don't reason with a rabid dog. You just fuckin' put 'em down."

XL grunted before cocking his gun. "We can't let them get away with this shit."

"And we won't." I growled as I traded glances with my family members.

"So, what's your call?" Ahsan questioned. "You're in charge now."

My chest deflated with a hard sigh. "I'm trying to avoid a fucking war, but I'm not afraid to go to the front lines if I have to."

XL nodded. "Then let's go. We need to catch these niggas before they disappear."

Ahsan heaved himself up to a standing position. "Or before they strike again."

"XL, put the word out on the streets. If they catch anybody outside of our organization selling our shit, I want they asses brought straight to me."

⁂

I turned the knob and stepped into my apartment, exhausted, frustrated, still in the same clothes I was in the night before. The three of us sat outside Jules's apartment all night until the sun came up, taking shifts to see if that nigga or any of the goons that helped him rob us showed up around her spot. Nothing happened.

My feet dragged into the kitchen, my steps heavy and snail-like. I dropped my keys on the counter with a loud clatter. All I wanted to do was have a drink, a blunt, and some undisturbed sleep in my bed. Hopefully, after some good rest, I'd find the clarity I desperately needed. How the fuck was I supposed to be the head of a fucking criminal organization, and I couldn't even do simple shit like ensure my product got to where it needed to go without any goddamn hiccups? I could feel all the power and respect I'd harnessed slipping through my fingers like smoke. If I weren't careful, our entire empire would come crashing down around me, and I'd be the one to blame. I wondered how many nights my brother had gone to bed stressed as hell and unsure of what to do next to ensure we stayed at the top of the food chain. *Heavy is the head who wears the crown.*

The minute I pulled the glass out of the cabinet, I saw Brandi sit up from the couch with a groggy look. "Nigga, where have you been? It's six thirty in the fucking morning."

"I know what time it is," I answered, already sensing her sour ass mood.

"So, where the fuck have you been? And don't lie and give me some bullshit ass excuse about working or whatever you're gonna say."

I sighed heavily. "I *was* working. Today... yesterday was a fucking nightmare. We got robbed, and I spent the whole fucking day dealing with that shit."

"And you couldn't bother to pick up the phone and call me to say that instead of having me up half the night worried about you?"

"Didn't you just hear me say I was dealing with bigger shit?"

She sigh-growled. "I'm sorry. Is there anything I can do to help?"

I snapped. "No, B. I just need some peace and quiet. Go back to sleep."

"My night wasn't all roses either, seeing as though I was up for hours worried sick about you and your whereabouts, but thanks for asking," she said sarcastically before sighing explosively.

I scoffed. *There she goes, having to be the star of the show as always.* "I'm sorry, B. All right?"

"Nothing says I'm sorry like jewelry. Maybe you could buy me that Cartier necklace we saw last week when I went shopping. It would really cheer me up."

I raised an eyebrow. "Seriously? Did you not hear me say we just got fucking robbed, and your spoiled ass is thinking about jewelry?"

"It's not like that," she said defensively. "I just thought it might make me feel better."

"Like your ass needs more jewelry, Brandi. Be forreal. I have bigger fucking problems right now." I barked.

She frowned. "Why the fuck do you always have to be so dismissive? It's just a small thing. It's not like I asked you to buy me a Wraith."

I sucked my teeth. "A small thing? I'm dealing with some fuckin' life or death shit, and you're worried about a necklace? You see the mothafuckin difference?"

"Fine. If that's how you feel, maybe you should've just stayed wherever the fuck you were at!"

"Maybe I will. Anything is better than standing around this bitch arguing with you."

I stormed out of the apartment, slamming the door behind me.

I SLOGGED MY WAY INTO THE HOTEL BAR AT SEVEN IN THE morning, my mind racing. Why the fuck did Brandi always have to make everything about her? We just had a major loss, and all she could fix her mouth to talk to me about was the new, expensive ass necklace she wanted. It was like she didn't even give a fuck about what I was going through. Every time there was some shit going on with me, she always found a way to turn it into something about her and whatever she needed. I understood she wanted to feel better after being stressed about my whereabouts all night, but why the fuck couldn't she see that I was barely keeping my shit together? *Ahsan was right. Maybe Brandi is more trouble than she's worth. I need someone who can support a nigga, not add to my daily stress.*

I waved down the bartender, a friendly-looking, middle-aged man, and ordered a glass of cognac neat. As soon as he set it down in front of me, I took a long sip of my drink, staring into the glass as I chugged down the liquor like it was water. *I need to figure this shit out. I can't keep living like this.*

I traded glances with the bartender as he wiped down the bar. "Rough start to your day?" he asked, sensing my fucked up mood.

I let out a hard sigh. "You have no idea."

He nodded. "Sometimes a drink helps. Sometimes it makes shit worse."

"My brother thinks my fiancée is more trouble than she's worth. And after the last half hour I've had, I'm starting to wonder if his ass is right."

"Well, it's your life, so only you can decide. But remember, money can buy you a lot of things. Peace of mind ain't one of 'em," he said wisely.

I dipped my chin in agreement. "Yeah, you're right. Cheers to you," I said, raising my glass to him.

Nerissa

I sat in the waiting room with my heart making pirouettes in my chest. It was the first time I'd get to see my baby. That thought filled me with joy. But as I looked around and saw other expectant mothers with their present partners alongside them, a tidal wave of loneliness washed over me. I couldn't help but wish I had someone to share the moment with. Someone to hold my hand and feel the same butterflies in their stomach as I did. But I'd chosen not to say anything to anyone, so I had to be strong for myself. *I'm more than capable of doing this on my own. This is about me and my baby. This is our moment.*

When the technician called my name, I took a deep breath and followed her into the room. I changed into a hospital gown before laying on the table. I tried not to squirm as the technician applied the gel to the wand and slowly inserted it inside me. My chest inflated with a deep breath as I tried to calm the drum of my heart.

"There's your baby," the technician announced.

I stared at the black and white screen and saw the tiny, flickering heartbeat. Tears welled up in my eyes. There it was—my baby. So tiny yet so powerful. "Wow."

Seeing my baby for the first time made everything feel more real. I was going to be someone's mother. But alongside the overwhelming joy bouncing around inside me, there was a noticeable ache of sadness. *Am I ready to do this alone? How will Amir react when I tell him?* Still, I knew I had to focus on the positive and not get bogged down with the things I couldn't control. *My motherhood journey might be challenging, but I can do this. I have no other choice.*

<hr>

AFTER WORKING MY SHIFT, I CHECKED INTO MY MANDALAY BAY hotel room, flying from Albuquerque to San Diego and then from San Diego to El Paso before landing in Vegas for the night. While in town, I agreed to meet with Demario later that evening at my hotel room after finishing up with my client. Since finding out I was pregnant, I'd been giving away and trading trips with other attendants to be able to take on more hair appointments. I'd learned not to take the early morning flights to help combat my morning sickness that started right around my eighth week.

Hours later, I stood behind my client, a middle-aged woman, putting the final touches on her traditional sew-in, when my phone buzzed on the table. I glanced at it to see a text from Demario.

Bro: *I'm downstairs.*

I smiled at my client before holding up the mirror to her. "All done! How do you like it?"

She cheesed, admiring the new look in her reflection. "Oh my goodness! It's perfect! I love it! I look like a brand-new woman, or at least ten years younger. Thank you so much!"

I smirked while gathering my tools to pack them up, while she paid me digitally. "I'm glad you like it. Thanks for your business! I have to wrap up now; my brother is waiting for me downstairs. If you need anything else, feel free to text me. And I hope to see you the next time I'm back in town."

She stood up. "Of course. Thanks again, and take care of

yourself!"

"Will do. Thank you!"

The client left, and I quickly texted Demario back.

Me: *Room 512. Come on up.*

A few minutes later, there was a knock on the door. I opened it to find Maree with a big Kool-Aid smile.

He leaned in to hug me. "Hey, sis! How are you?"

I smiled. "Hey, Maree. I'm good, just a bit tired. You know how it is."

He nodded. "Yeah. Listen, I wanted to thank you for helping me out with that loan. It meant a lot."

I waved him off with a smile as if my fifteen hundred dollar contribution was a drop in the bucket. "Don't mention it. I'm glad I could help you when you needed it."

He reached into his pocket and pulled out an envelope. "Well, I wanted to pay you back. And then some," he said before handing it to me.

I was hesitant to open the envelope but was surprised when I did. "Maree, this is double what I gave you! How in the hell did you manage to turn a profit so quickly?"

He smirked confidently. "Oh, you know, just some good business decisions and a bit of luck."

I raised a questioning eyebrow. "Really? In just a few weeks? Ain't nobody that damn lucky."

He shifted his eyes toward the ground. "Yeah, well, I got a big contract with a local car dealership. They loved my work, so the owner brought me in to detail all the new cars they bring in before they go out on the lot."

"Hmm, okay. If you say so," I replied, knowing better than to believe his ass.

There's no way his ass made that much money so quickly with just a car detailing business. He's probably back in the streets, doing some-thing illegal. But I can't deal with that right now. I need to focus on my baby and my health. Ignorance was bliss, at least until the baby was born. Besides, I was about to bring a whole life into the world. It wasn't like I didn't need the money.

"So, how's everything else?" he asked, changing the subject.

I smirked. "Actually, I want to talk to you about something." I walked over to my purse and pulled out an ultrasound photo to show him. "You're going to be an uncle!"

His eyes widened. "No fucking way! Are you forreal?"

"Yeah."

"Shit. That's wassup, Nerissa!" He congratulated me while looking at the photo. "Wow, look at that. How far along are you?"

"A couple of months."

"Who's the baby's father?"

I shook my head, unwilling to answer his question with the truth. "It's complicated."

"How complicated?"

"Complicated enough to where I don't want to ruin this happy moment, all right? I wanted you to be one of the first to know."

I never told Demario about Amir and had never told Amir about Demario. Speaking about my family wasn't something I shared with people, no matter how close they were to me. I preferred to keep some aspects of my childhood private. I didn't know why. Maybe a part of me was sensitive over how complicated our family ties were, especially since we had different mothers and didn't grow up together. My mother considered him a side baby and never saw eye to eye with his mother, so we only saw each other occasionally.

Aside from that, he was locked up when Amir and I met, and that was when we hadn't spoken for years. To be honest, I hadn't even considered building a lasting relationship with him until our father passed away. After losing my mother at sixteen and my father about a decade later, Demario was the only family I had left. Now that he was out, I felt protective of him and wanted to do my best to keep him in my life. If not for me, then for my unborn child.

"Well, I appreciate it. I'm glad you wanted to share that with me. I know we haven't been the closest over the years."

"Yeah. I know."

"I think this baby is a sign that you should come back to Vegas. And I don't mean these overnight pop-ins for work. I mean permanently. I'm out of prison and want to be there for you and my niece or nephew. You shouldn't be going through this alone."

"Who said I was alone?"

"I know what complicated means when it comes to a nigga not wanting to step up and take responsibility for the life he created."

Although it wasn't like that, I decided not to correct him. It was easier for him to think my child's father was a deadbeat. Maybe he wouldn't be so concerned with asking me more questions about it.

I shrugged. "I've been thinking about settling down after the birth, but I'm unsure where. Being closer to you would be nice, especially now that Dad passed. It would be like having a piece of him," I considered, knowing moving back to Vegas would give me the sense of family I'd been lacking for some time.

Maree smiled. "Exactly. We can look out for each other. I'm not saying you have to decide today, but think about it, okay?"

I nodded. "I will. And thanks for paying me back. This is going to help a lot with the baby."

"Say less. Anything you need, I got you."

Before I could reply, his phone rang. When he reached into his pocket to pull it out, I noticed a wad of cash sticking out. I sucked my teeth. As tempting as it was to move back to Vegas, I couldn't ignore the red flags. Maree's bullshit story about the money didn't add up. If he was back in the streets, did I really want to be around that?

He looked at the screen and then up at me. "Yo, I gotta head out."

I hugged him tightly. "Take care of yourself, Maree. And stay out of trouble, okay?"

He smiled. "Stay dangerous, sis. And don't worry about me. Life is good right now. I'll be fine."

I nodded. "I hope so. See you."

I watched as he strolled down the hallway with the phone glued to his ear. I closed the door and leaned against it as my mind filled with uncertainty. *Maybe moving to Vegas is the right choice.* But being back in Vegas full-time meant being privy to my brother's business dealings and being in the same city as Amir.

Seeing him with his soon-to-be wife would be emotionally draining, and I didn't want to get caught up in old feelings or unnecessary drama. I thought I was over him, but if life had shown me anything, being in the same city with Amir was bound to bring up old feelings. *Can I handle that emotional roller coaster while trying to raise a baby?*

Thinking about Amir always brought up a chain reaction of feelings inside me. On one hand, he was a big part of my life, and we shared some good times while we were together. But on the other hand, the emotional strain was taxing. Seeing him move on so quickly, especially with someone else, was still a hard pill for me to swallow. Besides, he was about to get married. How would she react? Would an unexpected side baby cause more drama than it was worth? I was already dealing with enough. Anything unnecessary wasn't welcomed in my presence.

I picked up my phone and scrolled to his Facebook page, thumb hovering over the messenger button. *Should I tell him about the baby? Part of me feels like he has a right to know. After all, this is his child too.*

But then I hesitated. I thought about how I didn't want to bring unnecessary stress into my life. *What if he reacts badly and pisses me the fuck off? What if he tries to get involved in a way that complicates this shit even more than it already is? But what if he wants to be a part of our child's life? Maybe he has changed. But you can't tell if someone changes in one night, right? Perhaps he would step up and be a good father.* It was all hard to know without giving him a real chance.

Besides, I needed all the support I could get. My brother made it clear he wanted to be there for me, and that was something I couldn't take lightly. Maybe there was a way I could keep enough distance from him to avoid worrying about having my nose in his business. It was a lot to consider, and I had to make the right decision with my and my baby's best interests in mind.

Amir

T*wo weeks later.*

Over the past couple of weeks, things had gone from sugar to shit. It started with the first three stash houses being hit. The loss was significant, but I managed to cover it up and fulfill my clients' needs. I tightened security, installed more cameras, and hired additional guards. When I thought things couldn't get worse, I received a call from XL. The same shit happened again. Another stash house hit, more product gone. I felt a sinking feeling in the pit of my stomach. It was like déjà vu but on a much larger and deadlier scale.

My clients were heads of gang organizations. They didn't appreciate the delays and missing work. They expected the forecast to call for snow in their cities, no matter where they were located. The complaints began to trickle in, causing my stress levels to soar. The complaints had turned into threats of taking their business elsewhere.

My entire reputation was on the line. I knew I couldn't keep the issue from Jefe any longer.

I poured over the security footage, trying to piece together a pattern, but nothing new emerged. The timing of the hits, the precision of the takedown, and the knowledge of where the security cameras were, all pointed to one conclusion. Like Rico and Bradley had done my brother, someone within my trusted circle was betraying me. Rico weighed heavy on my mind. I still dreamt about skinning that nigga alive when I caught him. Determined to get to the bottom of it, I called an emergency meeting with all my men.

"We have a mole," I told XL, my voice steady but filled with rage. "And nobody leaves until we find out who the fuck it is."

My cousin and I spent hours cross-referencing the times of the robberies with all our men. I discovered that only a select few were consistently on duty during each incident. This narrowed down the list of potential suspects. We interviewed every one of them. They all came up clean except one. Kenny was the only nigga that seemed unusually nervous and evasive when XL questioned him about his whereabouts during the robberies.

"We've seen the security footage, mothafucka," XL said, cocking his gun. "There's some shit that don't add up. Explain why you weren't on guard every time there was a hit at the houses you were supposed to be watching."

Kenny's caramel face turned white. He stammered, "I... I don't know."

"I'm not gon' lie to you. This shit ain't looking too good for you right now. You should save yourself the agony and come clean."

I grunted. "You know niggas talk, Kenny. And word around here is you've been making some large deposits to your bank account that coincide with the dates of the robberies."

"I–I–"

"Fuck it, XL. Let's blow this nigga's brains out."

Kenny's beady brown eyes darted around the room, searching for an escape. Sweat poured down his bald head. "Wait! Wait! Okay! I'll talk! Nigga, I swear, I didn't mean for this shit to happen. They threatened me. They said they'd hurt my family if I didn't help them get in."

"Who?"

"Nigga named Demario and some other goons. I don't know. They had mad guns and shit. I just had a kid, man. I couldn't take the risk. I'm sorry."

I took a deep breath, trying to control my anger. "Why didn't you come to me? We could have handled this shit together."

Kenny looked down at the pavement as if he were ashamed. "I was scared, man. I'm sorry. I didn't know what to do. I never wanted to betray you."

"And yet you did," I said before giving XL the nod of approval.

He handed me his gun to finish the job. I cocked it and grunted before pulling the trigger, watching Kenny's lifeless body hit the ground with a loud, final thud. "Bitch nigga."

I UNLOCKED THE DOOR TO THE APARTMENT, HOPING TO PICK UP some clean clothes. I'd been staying at a hotel since my last argument with Brandi, needing space to clear my head and find peace. The stress from the recent hits had been weighing heavily on me. And I wasn't in the mood to be around anybody. As I stepped inside, the sound of Brandi listening to music in the bedroom rose to my ears, and I braced myself for our face-to-face interaction. I entered the bedroom to find her dressed, clearly preparing to go out. She looked up, surprised to see me standing in the doorframe.

"Amir, what are you doing here?"

I looked her up and down. "I just came to get some clothes. Where are you going dressed like that?"

She was clad in a silver-gray sparkling sequined party dress that stopped at the middle of her thigh if that. The back was open, with only crisscrossed spaghetti straps holding her breasts and other assets.

"I'm meeting some friends for dinner. I didn't think you'd be back so soon."

I felt a surge of frustration roll through me. The robberies, the betrayal of another one of my men, and now seeing Brandi getting ready to go out while I'd been dealing with so much bullshit—it all came to a head.

I grunted. "Friends? Friends like who?"

She smacked her lips. "Bayleigh and Shante, if you must know."

"So, you gotta look like you sellin' pussy to get somethin' to eat now? Is that what we doing, Brandi?"

"Whatever, nigga. Fuck off. Ain't nobody ask for your opinion anyway."

"Must be nice to just go out whenever the fuck you want and have fun while everything around me is going to shit."

Brandi rolled her eyes, her tone turning sarcastic. "Oh, I'm sorry. I didn't realize I needed your permission to have a fucking social life. I guess I'm supposed to sit on the couch and twiddle my thumbs all day while you're out doing God knows what!"

"You wanna have a life when my business is literally being taken down from the fucking inside? I don't like the way you moving, Brandi. I don't fuck with it."

Brandi crossed her arms, her voice rising. "What the fuck is that supposed to mean? I'm moving the way I've always moved, nigga! Maybe if you actually talked to me instead of running off to a hotel, you'd know how worried I've been."

I scoffed. "Oh, poor Brandi. The world is so unfair to you. News-flash, baby girl: you're not the only one dealing with real fucking problems!"

Brandi stepped closer, her voice dripping with sarcasm as she shoved me. "Yeah, because yelling at me is going to magically fix everything, right, nigga?"

I clenched my jaw, realizing the argument was going no damn where. I quickly grabbed my clothes from the closet, stuffing them into a duffel bag. Without another word, I headed for the front door.

"Fine, just walk away! That's your solution to everything, isn't it?"

I paused for a split second, then left the apartment, slamming the door in my wake. I returned to my car and realized we still needed more time apart. The issues between us were too damn deep to be resolved in the heat of the moment. If I hadn't left when I did, I knew a case would soon follow.

AFTER LEAVING THE APARTMENT, I DROVE DOWN TO THE VEGAS Strip, seeking a distraction from all the bullshit and chaos in my life. The city's bright neon lights and high energy offered me an escape, no matter how brief. I found myself drawn to a strip club, the bass from the thumping rap music and bitches with ass spilling out of their G-strings standing on the street.

"Fuck it," I mumbled.

Inside, the atmosphere was hazy. Beautiful, exotic women of all colors and creeds performed on stage, their dazzling costumes and confident moves on the steel poles captivating the audience. I eased my joints at the bar, ordering a plate of chicken wings and two shots of top-shelf tequila. As I tossed back the shots and watched the show, I felt the weight of my frustrations lifting.

I pulled my eyes away from the stage long enough to look around. I was in a sea of pussy, surrounded by temptation. I battled with my dark thoughts. The idea of cheating crossed my mind more than once, a quick fuck to blow off some steam. But deep down, I knew getting my dick wet wouldn't solve shit. If anything, it would only add to my problems. Instead, I focused on my food, savoring the lemon pepper wings and washing them down with a cold beer. After finishing my meal, I decided to head back to my hotel room alone.

I lay in bed staring at the ceiling. The day's events replayed in my mind, but my thoughts soon drifted to someone else—Nerissa. I wondered what she was doing, where she was, and why she left without saying goodbye. I regretted fucking up in the past. Maybe we would still have been together if I had been more mature and willing to change. Instead, I was stuck in a toxic ass relationship with Brandi that was sucking the life out of me. No matter how hard we tried, we couldn't get things right. The arguments, the misunderstandings, the constant tension felt like a never-ending cycle, like hamsters on a wheel.

I sighed, feeling a deep sense of regret. I was sure there was no way in hell she and I were making it down the aisle. The thought of ending things with Brandi was painful, but I knew one of us had to be mature enough to call it quits for good. If not, the wheel would never stop spinning.

Nerissa

T*hree weeks later.*

I STEPPED OFF THE PLANE, MY HAND RESTING GENTLY ON MY small pudge. I'd officially made it to the beginning of my second trimester. Time was flying by. I felt comfort and nostalgia as I took in the familiar sights and sounds of Harry Reid International Airport. After retrieving my bag, I spotted Demario waiting at the arrivals gate. His brown face lit up when he saw me.

"Hey, sis! Look at you, glowing and shit. You look good."

I smiled. "Hey! Thank you. It's good to see you."

We shared a quick hug before heading to the car. "How was your flight?"

"It was cool."

"How long are you gonna be in town again?" he quizzed.

"I took off a couple of weeks from work just to look around for apartments and things."

"You seriously thinking about moving back out here permanently?"

I shrugged. "I'm considering it. I haven't entirely made up my mind yet. Are you sure it's cool that I crash with you? My airline doesn't cover my hotel stay when I'm not working."

"Yeah. You good. My place is nice. You'll like it. Plus, we've got the extra room."

"Hold up. We? Who's we? You got a roommate?"

"My girl, Jules."

"Y'all live together already?"

"Yeah. I moved in with her."

"You've been together for about thirty seconds, and you're already living together, let alone sharing bank accounts?"

"Hey, it paid off. You got your money back and more, right?"

"Yeah, I know."

"Okay, then. Relax, Rizzy. It's gonna be fine," he assured me.

Demario drove us to his place, which I'd just found out was actually his girlfriend's apartment. As we proceeded inside, I immediately noticed the spacious living room with large windows that let the natural light spill in. The eggshell-painted walls were adorned with a few abstract art pieces and quotes that added a pop of color and made the place feel more homey. A large, charcoal gray sectional dominated the center of the room, decorated with four Christian Dior throw pillows in various sizes. In front of the sofa was a sleek glass coffee table and a new sixty-inch flat-screen TV mounted on the wall with the open box next to it.

The open layout spilled directly into the kitchen, equipped with a high-end coffee machine and other stainless steel appliances, crisp white cabinets, and a burning sugar cookie-scented candle on the granite countertops. The kitchen island had a couple of bar stools around it. Everything was neat and in order. Overall, the apartment felt welcoming and well-kept. Still, I felt a bit uneasy.

"It's nice here," I complimented.

"Yeah. Jules keeps it real spic and span in this bitch."

"Yeah. I can tell. It's giving real posh domestication in here."

He picked up my suitcase. "Let me show you your room."

As I followed him down the narrow hallway and into the bedroom, I noticed the neatly made queen-sized bed dressed in soft, expensive-looking linens and a Chanel throw blanket at the foot. A small mahogany nightstand with a crystal lamp and a lavender-scented candle sat beside the bed, and a slim dresser next to an oversized wall mirror completed the space.

"Are you sure your girl is okay with me staying here? I seriously don't wanna intrude."

Maree wagged his head. "Don't worry. She's cool with it. Besides, you're family."

I nodded, but I couldn't shake the feeling of being a burden. Instead, I decided to bring up the other concern that had been pressing on my mind ever since I crept inside and noticed all the expensive ass things.

"Maree, how are you doing financially? I mean, I know you say things have been good with your detailing business, but... y'all are living quite well up in here."

He hesitated for a moment before responding. "We good. Everything is straight."

"What does she do for a living?"

"Well, she was a personal assistant."

"Was?"

"Yeah. She's looking for a new job. She's out on an interview right now. She should be back soon."

I sighed before taking my seat on the edge of the bed. "I mean, you've only been with her for a short time. Why are you already living together? You're not using her, are you?" I asked, halfway accusing him.

He looked a bit defensive, but then his expression softened. "Using her? She approached me, Nerissa. She was the one who wanted me to move in. I wasn't sure about it in the beginning, but a nigga needed a place to stay, and she insisted. She said she wanted to help me get back on my feet, so I took her up on her offer."

I studied him, trying to gauge his sincerity. "Okay. I just want to make sure you're not taking advantage of her kindness just because she has a stable situation. Relationships can get complicated, especially when you're blending your lives together so damn fast."

"I hear you, Rizzy. I mean, you sound like a hater, but I hear you."

"A hater?"

He chuckled. "Yeah. But it's cool. I care about Jules, and I'm not trying to use her. She's been holding a nigga down, and I appreciate that."

I nodded, feeling a bit more reassured but still cautious. "And what about all this expensive stuff in here? It's all from the car detailing? Nothing else?" I probed.

He groaned. "Goddamn, you nosy as hell."

"I'm nosey because I know your ass, Maree. Now tell me the truth. How y'all got all this nice shit when she don't have no job, and you just got your business off the ground?"

"I'm back doing my thing in the streets," he admitted. "But before you say anything, I'm being safe about how I go about my shit this time around. I promise you."

My heart pounded in my throat. I'd hoped he was done with that life for good, but deep down, I'd always known the truth.

"Damn, Maree. I was afraid of that. I guess I just wanted to believe things were different and that your hardheaded ass learned from your mistakes."

"I hear you. But I tried doing the straight and narrow shit, but nobody is out here eager to hire a fuckin' felon, Rizzy. You know that. So, I hit a couple of licks after I first got out. I thought I would get back with my ex, but that shit didn't work out. Her cousin was looking out for me where she could. She put me onto some quick cash, but I needed more. So, I had to do what I had to do. Then I met Jules, and everything started falling into my lap."

"What did you really spend the money I gave you on?"

"The less you know, the better."

I let out a loud sigh, feeling disappointment and frustration. I'd tried to ignore the signs, but now I had no choice but to face the reality. The game had its claws deep in my brother, and it wasn't letting up.

"Does she know?" I questioned.

"Know what?"

I sucked my teeth. "Don't play with me, Maree. Does Jules know how you're making your money?"

"She does."

"And she's good with it?"

"Look around this bitch, Rizzy. I don't see nobody complaining but you."

I felt a stab of guilt in my chest for trying to ignore what I already knew was true about my brother's situation. He was grown. I couldn't change his choices. His relationship wasn't any of my business, nor was his freedom. All I could do was support him as best as possible while maintaining a safe distance from his illegal dealings.

Suddenly, his phone rang. He pulled it out of his pocket and glanced at the caller ID before holding his finger to me, putting a pin in our conversation. He stepped into the hallway to take the call, but his voice carried back into the bedroom.

"Hey, what's up?"

"D, when are you gonna come through for me with some money? You know I need it," the woman on the phone said through the speaker. "You forgot I helped you when you needed it, nigga? The money I helped you steal from my cousin was for *both* of us. We had a deal, and my money is drying up!"

I perked up, my curiosity piqued. I quietly moved closer to the doorframe, trying to hear better.

Maree lowered his voice. "Chill, yo. I promise I got you, all right?

I ain't forgot what you did for a nigga, Z. You looked out for me, so I'ma look out for you. Besides, I know it's what my cousin would've wanted."

My eyes widened in shock. "Oh shit," I whispered before sliding my hand over my mouth.

"Thank you, D. I appreciate you."

"Say less. I'll get up with you later, all right?"

"Okay, I'll be waiting."

My brother hung up and turned around, startled to see me standing a few feet away. I looked at him with a mix of shock and anger on my face.

"Who the hell was that on the phone?"

"Damn, yo. Mind your fuckin' business, Rizzy."

"Tell me!"

He grunted. "It was Zyon. She was my cousin's girlfriend before he got killed."

"Your cousin who? All our cousins on Dad's side are grown as hell."

Demario sucked his teeth, annoyed with our conversation at every turn. "He was on my mama's side. He was in the game and got taken out. She was with him when that happened. That's all. End of story."

I narrowed my eyes. I didn't know his cousin or the woman from Adam, but I didn't like whatever shady dealings he had going on with her. "And what was that about staging a robbery at her apartment? You out here robbing niggas?"

"Chill. It wasn't like that."

"Then tell me how it was, Maree! I heard what you two said on the phone! What role did you play in that shit then?"

He shot his guilty eyes at me. "Look, I told you nobody was knocking down my door trying to hire me when I was released. I needed a quick come up, and she looked out. I'm going to pay her back, and we'll be straight. That was the fucking deal."

I shook my head. "I don't like this shit at all, Maree. At all! You need to be careful. I don't want your ass getting into any more trouble."

"I know, Nerissa. But I had no other choice. Just trust me on this."

"You know I just want you to be safe. You're about to be somebody's uncle. I don't want to see you go back to jail."

"I know, sis. I know this shit is not ideal, but like I said, I promise I'm being careful. I'm not going back to eating jail food again for nobody."

I nodded with a hard sigh. Demario would never tell me the whole story behind that woman's request for money and how he was mixed in with whatever janky ass plan they had. I worried about all the potential risks involved. The closer I got to my brother, the further away I wanted to get from Vegas altogether.

———

A COUPLE OF HOURS LATER, I WAS UNPACKING A FEW OF MY toiletries in the guest room when the sound of the front door opening seeped into my hearing. A few minutes later, my brother's girlfriend, Jules, walked in with a warm smile that showed a full grid of teeth.

"Hi, Nerissa! It's so nice to meet you in person finally."

I couldn't help but return a complimentary grin. "Hi, it's nice to meet you too. Thanks for letting me stay here."

"Of course! You're family. How about we go out for lunch and do some shopping? I'd love to get to know you better."

"Uh, yeah. Sure. That sounds great," I replied.

Just then, my brother walked in, looking in a hurry. "Hey, I gotta go handle some business. How'd your interview go?"

"It went well. I'm hoping to hear back something soon."

He kissed her forehead. "I know you'll get it, baby. But in the meantime, here's some cash for you two to go out to eat or shopping or something."

Jules giggled. "You read my mind, baby. We were just talking about getting out of here and getting to know each other."

"Bet. Enjoy that. And, Rizzy, don't be telling her no embarrassing ass stories about me either."

I smirked. "I can't make any promises."

I watched him hand Jules a wad of cash, kiss her on the cheek, and head out the door. Seeing the cash exchange reminded me of the reality I'd hoped wasn't true. On the one hand, I appreciated that my brother wanted to ensure we had a good time, but I knew where his money came from and what he had to do to get it. I couldn't help but worry that he could endanger himself and others.

"Well, looks like lunch is on my man today. Ready to go?"

I nodded before grabbing my purse. "Yeah, let's do it."

THE RESTAURANT PATIO WAS THE PERFECT SPOT FOR A RELAXING lunch. Our table for two was surrounded by lush greenery, with potted plants, hanging flower baskets, and string lights overhead. We sat shaded by large umbrellas that provided relief from the sun. We ordered our food—a grilled chicken salad with mixed greens and a light vinaigrette dressing for me and a plate of shrimp scampi served over a bed of linguine with a side of garlic bread for her.

As we waited for our food, our conversation flowed effortlessly, allowing us to get to know each other better.

"So, remind me how you and my brother met again? He told me you approached him."

Jules rolled her lips to contain a smile before taking a sip of her iced tea. "Yeah, that's right. We met at a mutual friend's barbeque. I noticed him right away and decided to strike up a conversation. We just clicked, you know?"

I nodded while trying to recall if their stories aligned. "He seems happy with you."

"Thanks. I'm happy, too. He came into my life when I didn't know if I'd ever find love again."

"So, you'd just recently gotten out of a relationship?"

"No. Well, not exactly. I had this... fling with my boss. It got super inappropriate, and I decided to part ways with the company. Hence, why I was at an interview today," she explained.

"Gotcha. Workplace romances are always risky."

"Yeah. But when I found Demario, I knew he was exactly the man I needed in my life. I really care about him."

"That's good. And because you care about him, I want to ask you something."

"What is it?"

"Are you aware of how my brother is getting his money?" I blurted out.

"You mean from his mobile car detailing business?"

I leaned in. "I mean his other business."

Jules paused, then nodded slowly. "I know he's involved in some things that aren't exactly legal if that's what you're saying."

"And you're okay with it?"

Her shoulders slumped as she sighed. "It's complicated."

"How?"

"It just is. But whatever your brother is doing, he's doing it to provide for us. But I won't lie and say I don't always worry about him."

"I get that. So, why don't you tell him to stop?"

"I've tried talking to him about finding a safer way to make money, but he's stubborn. He feels like the streets are the only way. Why are you asking me all this?"

I sighed. "Because I just found out some things recently, and it's got me worried about him too. I don't want him getting back into trouble, especially with me being pregnant."

Jules's face lit up with excitement. "Hold up. You're pregnant?"

"Yeah. He didn't tell you?"

"No! Congratulations! That's so exciting! How far along are you? Are you excited to be an expectant mother?" she probed, bombarding me with questions.

I shook my head, trying to process all her probes at once. "I'm in my second trimester. And to be honest, I'm still a ball of emotions. I'm excited about the baby, but I'm also nervous because a baby is a big fucking deal, you know? It's a big change."

"I can imagine. At least you don't have to do it alone, right? That's if you and the baby's father are on good terms."

I sighed. "It's complicated. We have a history, but things have been... distant between us as of late. He doesn't know about the baby yet."

"Oh shit. Why not?"

"I'm just taking my time trying to figure things out for the baby's sake and my sanity. But I don't plan to keep it from him forever."

"Do you know if you want a boy or a girl?"

I chuckled. "At this point, I just want a healthy baby. But if I had to choose, maybe a girl. What about you? Do you see yourself having kids with my brother someday?"

Jules cheesed. "Yeah, I do. I've always wanted to be a mom. And since things are so good with Demario and me, it's not hard to think about starting a family. Maybe not right now, but someday."

"I get that. But when the time is right, I'm sure you'll be an amazing mom."

"Thanks, Nerissa. And you're going to be a bomb-ass mother too! Your baby is lucky to have you, and they don't even know you yet."

I smiled. "Thanks. That means a lot."

Just as the waiter arrived with our food, I saw a familiar face walking toward us. It was Amir. I panicked the moment we locked eyes. It was as if we'd spoken him up. I wasn't prepared for another surprise encounter with him, especially in an unexpected public setting. My heart pumped ragged breaths, and I quickly backed away from the table and excused myself. I needed a moment to gather my thoughts and decide how to handle the situation. Seeing him brought up memories and unresolved feelings, making me realize just how much I still needed to process when it came to our future.

"Hey, I, uh, I'll be right back."

I pushed myself to standing and hurried away from the table, trying to avoid him. My mind raced with a million questions: *Why in the hell does he have to be here? What if he noticed my pudge and asks if I'm pregnant?* I felt a knot forming in my stomach, a blend of anxiety and panic about what running into him before I was ready could mean.

Amir

As I walked down the street, lost in thought, I spotted a familiar face sitting on a restaurant patio. I froze, making sure I was seeing what I thought I was. *It can't be her, can it?* My heart jerked against its tethers as I watched Nerissa race away from the table with a small pudge in her belly.

Curiosity and concern propelled my legs forward. The last time I saw her, she was naked and her stomach was as flat as a board. I raced inside the restaurant and caught up with her before she could dart into the women's bathroom.

"Nerissa?" I called out, my voice layered with surprise.

She froze in her step, turning to look at me with her eyes wide with shock. "Amir... hey."

I slowly approached her, my eyes never leaving her belly to make sure my eyes weren't playing tricks on me. "Is there something you need to tell me?"

She sighed, her shoulders slumping. "Fuck. I did not want this to be the way you found out I was pregnant."

"Am I the..."

"It's yours, Amir," she answered, cutting me off. "It happened that night in Phoenix."

My mind buzzed with alarm. "Phoenix was months ago, Nerissa! Why didn't you tell me? Why didn't you reach out?"

Her soft brown eyes filled with tears. "I was going to, then I saw your proposal video on Facebook. You're engaged, Amir? You still haven't learned your lesson about fucking around on bitches that love you?" she accused.

A flame of sadness ignited in my chest. She had it all wrong. "I wasn't engaged when I fucked you, Nerissa, and I'm not engaged now. We're done for good this time. I promise you."

"Listen, whatever messy shit that you've got going on, I don't want any parts of it," she said, tossing up her hands. "I didn't tell you because I didn't want to complicate things; a baby is the definition of complicated."

I sighed, still unable to process everything. "I–I don't know what to say. I just know we've got a lot of shit we need to talk about."

"I know, but now isn't the time or the place. I'm having lunch and need to return to my table."

"How long are you in the city for?"

"A couple of weeks."

"Then, please, can we at least exchange numbers? We need to talk about this further, Nerissa. I mean, damn. You're having my baby."

She nodded, handing me her phone. We exchanged numbers, and she turned to leave. Instead of letting her get away so quickly, I followed her outside to her table, where I saw the back of another woman's head. When she looked over her shoulder, my eyes widened in recognition. It was Jules, my brother's former assistant.

"What the fuck is going on here?"

Jules looked up at me, her expression riddled with shock. It was as if she'd seen a ghost. "Oh shit. I... I have to go," she stammered, standing up abruptly and leaving without taking another bite of her food.

As badly as I wanted to chase her down, I was more concerned with what Nerissa was doing with her. I turned my attention to Nerissa with confusion etched on my face. "How the fuck do you know that bitch?"

She hesitated. "Relax, Amir! She's my half-brother's girlfriend. I'm staying with them while I'm in town."

I blinked, almost unsure of what I'd heard. "Half-brother? You never told me you had a fucking half-brother, Nerissa. First, I find out you're carrying my kid, next I find out about some long lost family member I never knew you had. You're full of fucking secrets, Rizzy."

Her nostrils pushed out a hard sigh. "You're being dramatic. I never said anything about him because he was locked up while we were together. We weren't close back then, so in my eyes, there was nothing to tell."

"And you're close now?"

She shrugged. "Trying to be. I know our father would have wanted us to have a relationship now that he's gone and my brother's finally out of jail."

My curiosity piqued. "You got a picture of 'em?"

"What?"

"On your phone, Rizzy. Pull up his fuckin' picture."

She huffed before pulling out her phone and showing me a photo from his Facebook page. A sinister laugh escaped my lips. "You've got to be fucking kidding me."

"What? What's so funny, Amir?"

"Man, fuck!" I growled.

"Amir, you're scaring me. What the hell is going on?"

I glanced around, making sure we weren't drawing too much attention before I spoke. "My product has been getting stolen before it can be put on the trucks and shipped out. He's one of the niggas I saw on the security camera footage."

Nerissa's eyes widened in shock as she gripped both sides of the table. "Are you serious?"

"Dead serious. That bitch Jules used to work for my brother. She stole some information from us, and now I know for sure she gave it to your brother to fuck with our business."

"That's why she ran out of here like you were the ghost of Christmas past?"

"Exactly. And now I need you to tell me everything about your brother and what the fuck this nigga is up to because I'm not going to lie to you, Nerissa. That mothafucka is bad news, especially when it comes to my business."

"Oh my God. I had no idea, Amir! I swear!"

"I want to believe you, but had I not randomly seen you here, I wouldn't know about the baby that's been growing inside you for months. You can't blame me for wondering what other secrets you're keeping from me."

I had every right to be skeptical of Nerissa, her intent, and her connections to my rivals. But there was something about her aura that told me she wouldn't do a nigga like that. At least not intentionally.

She sighed. "You're right, and I'm sorry for not telling you. I know it sounds childish, but I saw that video and I completely shut down. I was just scared of getting my heart broken again."

As desperately as I wanted to talk to her about the baby and what we'd do about it, I couldn't even bother to process that over the revelation that my opp was also my baby mama's half-brother. My mind raced as I took a deep breath, trying to steady myself before I exploded. All the pieces had finally clicked, and it was a lot to fucking take in. Our web was more connected than we thought. Murdering the uncle of my unborn child was the last thing I thought I'd ever have to fucking do.

"We'll talk about all of this again soon, all right? I promise. But right now, I've got to go. Stay by your phone, all right?"

She nodded. "Okay."

LATER THAT NIGHT, XL, AHSAN, AND I SAT IN A CAR PARKED discreetly across the street from Jules's apartment. The dim glow of the streetlights cast a shadow across my face as I pulled out my phone to text Nerissa. Our brief interaction and bomb-dropping conversation had replayed in my head all day. We were waiting for her brother to leave so that we could run up on Jules, but I couldn't risk her safety knowing she was staying with them, too.

Me: *I'm at the Bellagio Fountains. Meet me to talk about the baby. It's important. Please come.*

Rizzy: *Okay. I'll be there soon.*

I watched intently as she stepped out of the building, feeling relief wash over me. I watched her get into an Uber, ensuring she was safely on her way to the hotel fountains and out of harm's way. My heart thundered in my chest from anticipating our conversation and the danger that lurked closer to home. Once she was out of sight, I glanced rearward to the apartment building. Her half-brother, Demario, was still inside. He'd crossed a line by robbing us, and I planned to get some answers, starting with Jules.

"Are you sure about this shit, nigga?" Ahsan queried, his voice low. "I know she told him she saw you today. He's gonna be waiting for us to pop out on him."

I nodded, my jaw set in a hard line. "I'm tired of waiting, especially now that we know they're connected. We need answers, and she's going to give them to us."

The tension in the car was thick enough to cut with a knife as we intently watched the building. I took a deep breath, knowing I needed to handle the situation carefully, not just for my own sake but for Nerissa and our unborn child. I couldn't risk fucking things up with her again. If I did, that would mean losing out on my child's life, and I didn't want that. I knew exactly what was at stake.

Finally, we saw Demario leave the apartment. We waited a few more minutes to ensure he was gone before getting out of the car and heading toward the building. The three of us moved swiftly and quietly, making our way to Jules's front door. Ahsan knocked, and after a minute, she answered it. The minute the door cracked open, we forced our way inside.

"What the hell are you doing here?" she screamed, eyes narrowed. "I'm not alone! I have company."

Ahsan pulled out a gun, pointing it straight in the center of her forehead. "Sit down and shut the fuck up, bitch," he ordered.

She froze. Her hands trembled as she slowly raised them in surrender. "Okay, okay. Just don't fucking shoot!"

XL immediately started a sweep of the apartment, checking each room, opening closets, and looking under beds. After a few minutes, he returned to the living room, shaking his head.

"She's lying. It's clear. There's no one else here," he confirmed.

Jules smirked, folding her arms across her chest. "Wow, XL, you always were the smart one, weren't you?"

I scanned her apartment, examining the details that screamed of sudden wealth. The living room was filled with high-end furniture, designer throw pillows that looked brand new, and a large, flat-screen TV mounted on the wall fresh out of the box.

My eyes narrowed as I took it all in. "Nice place. Looks like you've come into some money recently."

Her face flushed with guilt, her eyes darting away from mine. "It's not what it looks like," she stammered.

Ahsan shook his head, his grip tightening on the gun. "Oh, it's exactly what it looks like. Now, start fucking talking before I start redecorating this bitch with bullet holes."

"Cut the bullshit, Jules. We know you stole the book with the stash house locations, and we know you and your nigga have been stealing from us. Tell us where he went and how long he'll be gone!" I demanded, my voice cold.

Her eyes darted around, looking for an escape route. Suddenly, she made a break for the door.

"Don't let that bitch get away!" Ahsan shouted, lunging forward.

XL and I moved swiftly, blocking her path. XL grabbed her arm, dragging her back to the couch like a ragdoll without mercy. "Your ass ain't going anywhere," he growled.

Jules struggled, her eyes wide with fear. "Let me go! I didn't mean for any of this to happen!"

I stepped closer, my expression stern. "You need to calm down and start talking, Jules. Running won't help your ass now."

Her shoulders slumped in defeat, and she stopped struggling under XL's firm grasp. "Okay, okay. I'll tell you everything. Just please, don't hurt me."

Ahsan nodded before slightly lowering his gun. "We don't want to hurt you, Jules. We just need the truth," he explained, his voice softening slightly.

"I don't know."

Ahsan released the safety on the gun, itching to pull the trigger. He stepped forward, his voice low and threatening. "Don't make this harder than it needs to be. Just tell us where he is."

Jules laughed bitterly. "Harder? This is nothing compared to dealing with your rejection, Ahsan. I don't know where he is, and even if I did, why the fuck would I tell you?"

XL gripped her by the throat. She gasped for air, trying to come up with an excuse. "He–he had to make a run. He said he'd be back i-in a c-couple of hours."

Ahsan nodded, satisfied with the answer for the meantime. Jules gripped her throat and coughed, trying to refill her depleted lungs. He kept her at gunpoint while XL and I searched the apartment for the missing product or any money we could find. We moved quickly, checking every nook and cranny of the two-bedroom apartment.

In the second bedroom, I opened up the nightstand drawer and froze. There, by itself, was an ultrasound picture. My heart thieved an extra few beats as I read the name on it—Nerissa Barnes. Instantly, I knew I was looking at my baby. Without thinking, I quickly ripped off one of the pictures and slid it into my back pocket as my mind raced all over again.

"*Found it!*" XL shouted from the master bedroom.

I finished the distance into the hallway to see him coming out of the bedroom with two of our bricks of cocaine in hand. "I found them in the ceiling tile in the bathroom."

I nodded, relieved that we were on the right track. "Stupid ass nigga should know not to shit where he eats."

My brother kept his eyes trained on Jules. "I trusted you, Jules, and I'm usually a pretty good judge of character. Why the fuck would you do this?"

Her eyes darted around the room at the three of us. "I... I did it for revenge," she admitted. "I wanted to get back at you for choosing Sienna over me."

Ahsan's eyes narrowed. "So you got with my girl's ex-boyfriend to get back at me?"

She nodded, tears streaming down her face. "Yes. And I gave him the book because I knew it would hurt you like you hurt me."

I shook my head. "This is fucked up, Jules. You put a lot of mothafuckas in danger."

She sobbed. "I'm sorry, Ahsan! At first, it was just to get back at you, and then when he wanted to get back at Sienna, too, it just felt right. I didn't think it would go this far!"

"Just how far has it gone?"

She looked up at me with a sinister grin. "He said he's just getting started."

Before she could go into any detail, Demario returned to the apartment. As soon as the door opened, Jules yelled, "Run, baby! They're here!"

Hearing the warning, her boyfriend quickly turned and fled, escaping us just in time. The three of us charged down the stairwell behind him. I paused to pull out my gun. My finger hovered over the trigger as my breath steadied. It was the moment I'd been waiting for —to take down the mothafucka who'd been stealing from me and causing chaos in my life. But as I stood there, something inside me shifted. My grip on the gun tightened, my thoughts racing at a dangerous level. *I know I should pull the trigger and waste this nigga once and for all. But I can't.* I couldn't bring myself to kill the brother of the woman I once loved, the woman I still had feelings for, especially since I knew she was carrying my seed.

My seconds of hesitation cost me. Demario bolted down an alley and disappeared into the night.

"Fuck," I cursed under my breath, lowering my gun.

I knew I'd let my emotions get the best of me, and the nigga had slipped through my fingers like sand because of it. I stood there for a moment, the weight of my decision pressing down on me. I couldn't let that shit happen again. The last thing I wanted to do was break Nerissa's heart again by killing her brother. I was going to have to find another way to deal with Demario's ass, one that doesn't involve crossing a line I couldn't uncross when it came to Nerissa. With a heavy heart, I headed back to the car with the ultrasound picture burning a hole in my pocket. Things were far from over, but I had to regroup and figure out my next move.

Back in the car, the three of us sat in tense silence. Finally, I broke the quiet. "I need to tell y'all something."

"Does it have anything to do with why your ass froze out there?" My brother asked.

I sighed before pulling the ultrasound from my pocket and showing it to him. "Remember I told you I ran into my ex in Phoenix a couple of months back? Well, she's pregnant, and she's also Demario's half-sister. That's why I couldn't pull the trigger. I'm scared as hell to fuck things up with her again, especially when she's carrying my baby."

Ahsan and XL exchanged surprised glances. "Wait, what?" Ahsan queried.

"Yeah," I continued, "I couldn't make this shit up if I wanted to."

XL grunted before he and Ahsan paused, then broke into slow grins. "This shit is wild as hell, but congratulations, nigga!" XL said, clapping me on the back. "How do you feel about becoming a father?"

My tight chest expanded with a deep breath as the reality of the crazy situation sank in for the first time. "Honestly, I hadn't thought about it until now. It's... overwhelming as hell to think about, but also kind of exciting."

Ahsan nodded, a thoughtful look on his face. "This shit is a big deal, Amir. Congratulations! You know we're here for you."

XL chimed in. "Yeah, man. If you need anything, just let us know. We got you."

Ahsan's expression turned from jovial back to serious. "Because of the baby, I'll take care of Jules's boyfriend for you. You don't need that stress on your heart."

I shook my head. "I appreciate it, but I need to handle this myself. I don't want you getting involved any more than you already are."

Ahsan sighed but nodded in agreement. "All right, but if you need backup, you know where to find me."

I smiled, feeling a sense of relief and support from the closest niggas to me. "Thanks. You niggas are appreciated. I mean that. I love y'all."

XL patted me on the back again. "We love you too."

Nerissa

I stood by the Bellagio Fountains, my eyes nervously scanning the crowd. I checked my phone repeatedly, but there had been no message or call from Amir since he'd asked me to come to the fountains to talk. *Why did I even bother coming here? I should've known better than to believe he'd show up. This is so typical of his ass.* I glanced at my phone for the one-hundredth time. *He said he'd be here.* As the minutes ticked by, my frustration only grew. *I can't believe he's doing this to me again. Doesn't he care about me or the baby at all?* After waiting for over an hour, I left, feeling hurt and frustrated as fuck for having wasted my time and gotten my hopes up only to be let down.

The next day, my phone rang. Of course, it was Amir. My initial reaction was anger. *Oh, now he decides to call. What bullshit excuse is he going to give this time?* I glared at the screen, watching it ring until my voicemail kicked in. He called again. I ignored it. On his fifth call, I finally picked up.

"Oh, look who finally decided to call. What happened to you last night, Amir? Did your ass get lost on the way to the fountains?"

I wanted to hear what he had to say, but I refused to make it easy for that nigga.

"Nerissa, I'm so sorry. Something came up, and I couldn't make it. Please, let me explain," he begged, sounding remorseful.

"Explain?" I snapped. "Your ass didn't even bother to text or call me! I waited for your ass out there for over an hour, looking like a fucking dummy!"

"I know, and I'm sorry. Just give me a chance to make it up to you."

I sighed. "Make it up to me? Why, Amir? You can't even be straight up with me and tell me what was so important that your ass couldn't show up!"

"I can't explain all that right now, but please, trust me. Give me another chance to make it right."

My anger bubbled up. *He's sorry? That's it? His ass doesn't even have the fucking decency to tell me why he stood me up!* My skepticism deepened. *Why should I waste my time trusting his ass? He's let me down time after time in the past.*

I rolled my eyes as a sarcastic chuckle slipped from my lips. "Trust? *You?* That's real rich coming from you, nigga. But fuck it. I guess I'll show you how it's done and be the bigger person once again. I have a doctor's appointment with my new ob-gyn tomorrow. If you want to make it up to me, be there. Afterward, maybe we can talk about the baby and how we'll co-parent if I feel up to it."

"Send me the address, and I'll be there, Rizzy. I promise."

Mentioning the doctor's appointment brought up more feelings of hope and doubt. If he showed up, it would mean he cared. But could I count on him?

I smacked my lips. "We'll see about that. Your ass should stop making promises you can't keep!" I warned before hanging up.

After the call ended, an unanticipated wave of sadness washed over me. Despite wanting him at the appointment, my insecurities plagued my mind. *What if he didn't show up last night because he ran back to his fiancée? What if he comes to the appointment and realizes being a father is all too much for him?* I knew I shouldn't have been upset, but I couldn't help it. I wasn't in control of my hormones.

A small, nagging part of me wanted to believe him, but I couldn't keep setting myself up to get hurt. Falling for Amir and agreeing to trust him again felt like Charlie Brown repeatedly falling after Lucy moved the football away. But I needed to know if he would be around for the baby's sake.

My thoughts were transferred back to my phone when it rang again. This time, it was from an unknown number. I answered it with skepticism in my tone.

"Hello?"

"Hi. Can I please speak to Nerissa Barnes?"

"Speaking. Who is this?"

"Hello, Ms. Barnes. I'm Kelly Weideman with Desert Bay Apartments. We recently received your rental application. I'm calling to let you know we have a two-bedroom apartment on the third floor in your price range becoming available in the next two weeks. Are you still interested?"

My heart pranced in my chest. After looking around the city, I'd put in a few online rental applications. I never thought I'd hear back so soon. *Maybe this is the change I need—a new place closer to family and a new beginning for me and the baby.*

"Yes, I'm still interested. I'll take it," I replied.

"Awesome. Drop back by the leasing office to review the paperwork, and I'll get you your exact move-in date."

I smiled. "Thank you. I'll be there within the next hour."

THE NEXT DAY, AMIR AND I SAT IN THE WAITING ROOM OF THE ob-gyn's office. I kept my body language closed off, feeding into the nervous, tense energy between us. I stole a quick glance at him. He had on a simple, crisp black T-shirt and denim jeans. His ears, neck, and wrists were iced out with gold and platinum Cuban link chains, a diamond-encrusted watch, and at least twenty karats in each ear. As blinged out as he was, he looked nervous but determined to prove me wrong.

While we waited to be called back, Amir tried to engage in small talk with me. "So, how have you been feeling? Any morning sickness or cravings?"

"Oh, you know, just the usual. Craving accountability and honesty," I said dryly, being sure to hit him with short, sarcastic jabs every chance I got.

He winced but didn't retaliate with negativity. Deep down, we both knew he deserved it. Before he could ask me another question, the nurse called my name.

"Nerissa, the doctor will see you now."

We followed the nurse into the examination room. I sat on the examination table with my arms crossed over my chest, completely guarded. I glanced at Amir, who stood guard near the door. He nervously shifted his weight from one foot to the other, trying to catch my gaze, but I avoided all eye contact as best I could. Before he had the chance to try and strike up a conversation with me, there was a knock on the door. I exhaled a sigh of relief when the doctor stepped in. She was a middle-aged woman of South Asian descent. From the top of her chestnut brown head to the purple Crocs on her feet, she stood at about five feet six. She wore her crisp white lab coat with pride and had a calm, reassuring presence that I appreciated.

"Good morning, Nerissa. I'm Doctor Reed. How are you feeling today?"

I forced a smile. "I'm fine, thank you."

"Great. I've reviewed the medical records your doctor sent over from New York, and I have some exciting news. We can determine the baby's gender through a blood test today if you'd like to know."

I glanced at Amir, then back at the doctor, unsure if I wanted to share that moment with him, especially since I still felt a way about being stood up.

"I think I'd like to wait. It's a big decision, and I just want to be sure. Is that okay with you?" I asked Amir.

He nodded. "Whatever you want. I'm just glad to be here."

His words made my heart soften slightly, but I remained guarded. *He's here now, but for how long?*

Doctor Reed nodded while smiling warmly. "That's perfectly fine. We can revisit the decision later. Let's proceed with the regular checkup and take a look at your little one. Dad, you can come closer if you'd like."

He hesitated but stepped forward, standing beside me. He looked down at me, but I twisted my neck toward the screen to avoid his gaze. Doctor Reed applied the cold gel to my belly and began the ultrasound. Soon, the dark room was filled with the soft, rhythmic sound of our baby's rapid heartbeat.

She pointed to the screen. "There it is. That's your baby's heartbeat."

Amir's eyes widened as he heard the sound for the first time. He stared at the screen, unable to tear his eyes away. "Wow. That's really... *our* baby," he whispered.

My hardened expression softened, and my anger momentarily melted away as I watched the genuine emotion on his face. It was the same feeling I had seeing the ultrasound for the first time. I drew in a deep breath, feeling a mix of emotions. *This is it, Nerissa. Either he's going to stay, or he's going to run.*

"Yeah, that's our baby," I said softly as tears welled up in my eyes.

All my thoughts were silenced when he reached out and gently took my hand. I froze but never pulled away. For the first time, in what felt like forever, Amir and I shared a moment of connection, brought together by the tiny heartbeat of the life we'd created.

"Everything looks good. The baby is healthy, the heartbeat is strong, and you're doing great, Nerissa."

I smiled. "Thank you, Doctor."

As the doctor concluded her examination, we left the office. Amir spoke up as we reached the parking lot.

"Listen, I know you're still upset and have every right to be. But I'm here now, and I want to be involved. Can we at least try to talk about the baby and our plans?"

I sighed, exhausted from holding up my emotional wall. "Fine. We can talk, but don't expect me to forget what happened. This is about the baby, nothing else."

He dipped his chin. "I understand. Thank you for giving me another chance."

Maybe he does want to be a present father. But can I really trust him? I guess only time will tell.

THREE DAYS LATER, I WAS SITTING ON THE COUCH INSIDE JULES and my brother's apartment, scrolling through my phone, when Demario raced through the front door and slammed it behind him.

I cut my eyes at him, already sensing something was off. "Where the hell have you been? I feel like I haven't seen you in days."

"That's because I ain't been around," he answered, sounding rushed. "I been handling some business."

"Oh..."

"Listen, I'm only here because I need to pack some clothes, and then I need you to do me a favor."

"Pack? Where are you going?"

"Chill with all the questions, all right? Can you drive me to the airport?"

Sadness uprooted my heart. I knew exactly what he meant. He'd gotten himself into trouble *again*.

"What the hell is going on? Why do you need to go to the airport?"

"It's just business. I need to lay low for a while," he said evasively.

I sighed, frustration bubbling up inside me. *Here we fucking go again.*

"Business, huh? Don't you mean trouble? I already know you've been into some fucked up shit, Maree!" I accused, recalling the conversation Amir and I had at the restaurant.

I didn't like the fact that Amir was just as deep in the game as my brother was trying to be, if not deeper. It wasn't the type of life I wanted for either of them, but I knew I couldn't change them and it would be a waste of time trying.

"It's nothing I can't handle. A nigga just needs to get out of town for a bit."

"And Jules? What about her? You're just going to pack up and disappear on her?"

He hesitated. "I told her we had to cool it for a while. It's better this way."

I shook my head, feeling the stress building. *His ass will never learn.*

"Where are you flying to?"

"I'm not sure yet. I'll figure it out when I get there. Don't worry, sis. I'll reach out to you when I land on my feet."

My lungs filled with a deep breath before slowly exhaling. I couldn't change his mind and wouldn't waste my time trying. His leaving was probably the only way to keep him safe.

"All right, I'll drive you. But you need to be careful, okay? And keep in touch."

"Thanks, sis. I owe you one."

"Yeah, you damn right you do."

"I'll be ready to go in fifteen minutes," he assured me.

As my brother disappeared down the hall, I felt a knot of worry growing in my stomach. *I hope he knows what the hell he's doing, but he probably doesn't have a fucking clue.*

Amir

A flood of emotions washed over me as I sat in my car. I felt awe, fear, and an overwhelming sense of responsibility. Seeing the baby on the screen made everything feel real. The baby's heartbeat was so tiny, yet it carried the weight of a future I wasn't sure I ever imagined for myself. It was the first time my heart had swelled with a love I didn't know I could feel. But beneath the joy and pride, there was a gnawing anxiety eating away at my gut. Growing up, I never had a father figure in my life. I remembered the nights Big Mama rocked me to sleep because I was crying and wishing for a father that would never fucking come.

How the fuck can I be a good father when I don't know shit about having one? The question haunted me, echoing in my mind like a broken record. As waist-deep in the game as I was, I worried about repeating the cycle, about not knowing how to be there for my seed in the ways that mattered most. Most of all, I feared failing, not just Nerissa again, but the tiny life growing inside her that was half mine.

Despite our differences and the anger and resentment I knew Nerissa felt toward me, I wanted to be there for her and our child. And that meant letting things between Brandi and me fizzle out for good. I didn't want to hurt her, but our relationship had been toxic for too damn long. If anything, Nerissa's pregnancy was a sign that I needed to make a significant change in my life. I felt a shift within myself. It was time to move forward and be the father my child deserved. I made a silent vow to be present, love my kid unconditionally, and end the absence cycle that marked my childhood.

———

A FEW HOURS LATER, I STEPPED INTO THE APARTMENT WITH MY heart feeling like it was ready to claw its way out of my chest. Brandi was in the living room, scrolling through her phone with the TV on blast.

I cleared my throat. "Yo, B. We need to talk."

Brandi looked up, sensing the seriousness in my tone. She put her phone down and turned down the TV volume before giving me her undivided attention.

"What's going on?"

I took a deep breath before sitting down next to her. "There's something I need to tell you. It's about my ex, Nerissa. She's pregnant, and the baby is mine," I blurted out all in one breath while I had the nerve to say it.

Brandi's eyes widened in shock, and she immediately jumped to conclusions, just like I knew she would.

"Nigga, your trifling ass cheated on me? I knew you was living foul. Doing me dirty while I'm over here cooking, cleaning, sucking, and fucking you just how you like it. Nigga, I'm heaven sent! How could you fumble your blessing like this?"

I swung my head in a sharp no. "No, Brandi, I didn't cheat. It happened when we were on a break. It was just one time, but now there's a baby involved, and I gotta do the right thing."

"Tell me how many times you fucked that bitch!" she demanded, her eyes flashing with anger. "When did it happen?"

I ran my hand over my head, frustration etched in my knitted brow. "I just told you we were on a break and it was one time, all right? We weren't together when it happened. I—"

She cut me off, her voice sharp as a blade. "I always knew your ass couldn't be faithful!"

"It was just once!" I reiterated, my voice rising with every exchange. "We weren't together, Brandi. I *didn't* cheat on your ass! Damn!"

Her expression hardened, the hurt in her eyes refusing to dissolve. "I don't give a flying fuck if we were on a break, a separation, a cooling-off period, whatever. The fact that you couldn't wait to go out and get some pussy and was so fuckin' sloppy that you got the jump-off pregnant while I was here trying to pick up the pieces of whatever the fuck this is!"

"I'm sorry," I interjected with remorse. "I swear I never meant for this to happen. I wasn't going out there with intentions of fucking nobody. It just happened."

She shook her head, tears welling up but refusing to fall. "You don't get it, nigga. This changes everything! You had a baby on me! This isn't something I can just forgive and forget. How the hell am I supposed to trust your black ass now?"

I stepped closer, reaching out, but she backed away, her arms crossed defensively. "Please, just listen—"

Brandi's expression shifted from shock to anger, to something even more desperate. "So what?" she asked, her voice breaking. "You think you can just leave me for some bitch from your past, nigga? Is that it? Tell that bitch she can't have her old life back."

"No, it's not like that. I want to be there for my child. I need to be a present father, something I never had growing up."

Brandi's eyes filled with tears. I expected her to fly off the handles, curse, and scream, but she surprised me with her following words.

"I love you, Amir. I don't want to lose you, baby. You're mine, and I'm willing to stay through this *if* you can promise not to have anything to do with that bitch. We can stay together and raise the baby without her."

My brows screwed lower as I shook my head. "Brandi, that's not realistic. Nerissa is the baby's mother, not you. I can't just cut her out of our lives and the baby's life. I need to be involved in my child's life, which means being in contact with Nerissa whenever, wherever."

Brandi's face hardened, and she stood to her feet, her voice trembling with anger. "So you're choosing that bitch over me?"

I sucked my teeth. "I'm choosing to be a father. I'm sorry, Brandi, but I can't stay with you under those conditions. It's not fair to anybody."

Her vengeful eyes flashed with disgust and betrayal. She reached for the engagement ring wrapped around her finger and yanked it off before throwing it at my head.

"Fine. Take your ring and get the fuck out!"

I caught the ring midair, feeling a blur of sadness and relief. I pushed myself to standing and looked at Brandi one last time.

"I really am sorry shit had to end this way."

"Fuck you and that bitch, Amir!" she spat.

With that, I left the apartment, the weight of my decision settling in. I knew that shit wasn't going to be easy, but I was glad I got up out of there without being escorted out in cuffs or, worse, a body bag.

I put the phone up to my ear, calling Nerissa as I stepped into my hotel room. With a sigh, she finally answered on the third ring.

"Hello?"

"Hey. Wassup? You busy?"

She pushed out another heavy sigh into the receiver. "What do you want, Amir? I'm about to go to sleep."

"I was hoping we could talk. I need to see you."

"I thought I told you we don't have shit to talk about outside of the baby."

"Please, Nerissa. I ended things with Brandi. It's over. I want to show you I'm completely committed to our baby now."

"Good for you, Amir. But that doesn't change anything between us."

"Rizzy, please. I wanna be there for you and the baby. Can't we at least try to talk this shit out?"

She sucked her teeth. "I said no, Amir. We're parents to the baby and nothing else," she stated firmly.

Before I could say anything more, she hung up. My arm dropped to my side, feeling heavy as I wrestled with a mix of frustration and sadness. *Why does she always make shit so complicated?* I put my phone down and tried to focus on something else, but nothing would tear my mind away from Nerissa and our baby.

Nerissa

Four weeks had passed since I last saw Amir. During that time, I'd been busy settling into my apartment, which meant having my belongings shipped from New York back to Vegas and decorating until the place felt like my own. I hadn't heard from my brother or Amir, appreciating the space and time to focus on myself. However, I was headed to my sixteen or twenty-week OB-GYN appointment, and Amir had insisted on tagging along.

I spotted him sitting in the waiting room as I passed into the small office. He looked different—better, even, if that were even possible. His fresh haircut and crisp hairline framed his face perfectly, and his expensive cologne subtly filled the space between us. It was a comforting scent that I wouldn't have been able to stomach during my first trimester.

I took my seat beside him, and we exchanged polite greetings. There was a touch of awkwardness between us at first, as if we were strangers who'd seen each other around once or twice. We fell into a comfortable silence as we waited for my name to be called. I glanced around, noticing the other expectant mothers and their attentive partners, and then turned my attention back to Amir. I'd appreciated the space he'd afforded me over the past few weeks, allowing me to settle into my new apartment and process everything on my terms as my body grew. Yet, seeing him in the flesh, I couldn't deny my lingering feelings for him. There was a warmth in his presence that I'd missed.

"So, how's life been?" I asked, breaking the silence between us.

"It's been hectic but manageable," he replied, leaning back in his chair. "How about you? You all settled into your spot?"

"Yeah. I like it. It's nice," I said as a smile breezed over my lips. "It's starting to feel like home. I finally unpacked all the boxes, so it's about eighty percent there."

"That's wassup," he said, nodding. "I know moving sucks. Let me know if you need any help with anything, especially for the baby's room."

I shook my head. "No, I think I've got it under control. But thanks for offering."

There was a brief pause in our conversation before he spoke again. "Have you been feeling okay? Any morning sickness or anything?"

"Not too bad. There are just bits of nausea here and there if I eat something too spicy, but it's manageable. It's nowhere near as bad as it was in my first trimester. The cravings are starting to kick in, though."

He chuckled. "Cravings, yeah? Anything in particular, y'know, besides accountability and honesty."

I giggled, noticing what he'd done. "Clever. If I tell you, you can't judge."

"I won't. I promise."

"Bacon and ice cream... together," I admitted as laughter charged out of me. "It sounds crazy, but I can't get enough of it."

He grinned. "Well, if you ever need a nigga to make an ice cream run for you, I got you."

I appreciated his jovialness and his effort to keep the conversation from falling flat. It felt good to talk about small, everyday things, even if only for a moment. Before our chat could continue, the nurse called my name. We both stood up, and he placed a reassuring hand on my lower back as our feet took us toward the examination room. The small talk had helped ease some of the underlying tension between us, causing me to feel a little more at ease.

During the examination, I lay on the table with my shirt pulled up to expose my growing belly. Doctor Reed applied the cool gel and began the ultrasound. As before, our ears perked up to the rhythmic sound of our baby's heartbeat. I watched Amir's eyes light up with joy.

"Is that the head? Or it's... y'know?" he asked, pointing his index finger at the monitor.

I chuckled, somehow finding amusement in him trying to decipher one of the baby's body parts from the other. His genuine curiosity and excitement made my heart tip over. Moments like that made me think of the future, despite the uncertainties ahead. The doctor smiled and guided him through the image, explaining what we were seeing.

"You're measuring right around sixteen weeks," the doctor said. "I can tell you the sex of the baby if you'd like."

I looked at him, pinning him with a serious lens. "I still want to wait," I said softly, hoping he understood.

He nodded, a loose smile playing on his lips. "Me too."

"Thank you."

I was relieved that he agreed to wait. It showed me that he respected my wishes and was willing to be patient.

As we left the office, I couldn't shake the feeling that, despite everything, the bond between Amir and I was still there. I wondered if we'd ever be able to repair our relationship and become friends, not just for the baby's sake but because no matter how badly I tried to deny it, there was still a special place for him in my heart.

My stomach growled as Amir led me across the parking lot toward my car.

"When's the last time you ate?" he quizzed, side-eyeing me.

"You heard that?"

"Let me treat you to lunch."

I declined with a quick swipe of my head. "Don't worry about me. I can grab something at home."

"I'm for real, Rizzy. I got you. Whatever you want. You want ice cream? You got it. You want Hawaiian pizza and brownies? Say less. It's your world."

"Okay, then," I agreed.

We found a cozy Italian restaurant nearby and settled into a booth.

He picked up the menu before flashing a sly grin at me. "Anything making your mouth water?"

I scanned the options, feeling more relaxed now that we were away from the doctor's office. "I think we're in the mood for the chicken Alfredo."

"We?"

"Me and the baby, duh."

He chuckled. "Good choice. I might go for the steak with a side of spaghetti. I haven't had a good meal in a minute."

We placed our orders and handed the menus back to the waiter. As we waited for our food, Amir leaned back in his seat, looking at me with genuine interest in his brown orbs.

"What?"

"Nothing."

"Tell me."

He smirked. "I don't know why, but I was randomly thinking about that time you tried to bake me a cake for my birthday," he recalled with a playful smile hanging on his lips.

I giggled, nodding. "Yikes. How could I forget? I damn near destroyed an entire kitchen trying to make a cake from a box."

He laughed alongside me. "I walked in and saw fucking flour everywhere except in the damn bowl."

I giggled. "I still don't know how that happened, but I had fun *attempting* to make it."

"Yeah, and we ended up ordering pizza and putting birthday candles in my slices instead," he said, shaking his head with a cute grin. "That was the best birthday I ever had."

I smiled, feeling a warm sense of nostalgia. "I'm positive I've never laughed that much or that hard before."

"Me either."

After a brief pause, I decided to share something more recent and special. I wasn't sure why, but being with him felt natural, almost like the past few years of distance hadn't happened.

"I felt the baby move for the first time last week," I shared.

His eyes widened with excitement. "Forreal? What was that like?"

"Weird, but still exciting," I said, my voice light with joy. "I was lying on the couch, watching TV, and suddenly, I felt this little flutter in the pit of my stomach. I sat up because, at first, I wasn't sure what it was, but then it happened again. It was like a tiny tap from the inside, like the baby was saying, '*Hey, mom, it's me.*'"

"Wow. I bet that shit was so dope."

"It was," I agreed. "I just sat there, feeling this little life we created moving around inside me. It made everything feel crazy real, y'know?"

He nodded as a soft smile formed on his face. "I wish I could have been there to feel it too."

"Well, we've plenty of time for that. I'm sure you'll get to feel the baby kick soon."

He reached across the table to squeeze my hand, his eyes meeting mine with a look of anticipation. "I can't wait."

After lunch, we decided to go shopping for the baby. We wandered through the high-end baby store, picking out adorable gender-neutral outfits and essentials for the baby's room. I marveled at how tiny everything was.

"Look at these," he said, holding up a tiny pair of Gucci baby shoes. "I can't believe how small they are."

I laughed, nodding. It was as if he could read my mind. "Aren't they the cutest things you've ever seen?"

"They are. The baby is going to look so fly in them."

We moved from aisle to aisle, selecting important essentials like soft baby blankets and car seats. He seemed to be having the time of his life, enthusiastically picking out items.

"What about this?" he asked, showing me a polar white Baby Dior teddy bear.

"Definitely," I said, smiling. "Every baby needs their favorite teddy bear, right?"

As we continued shopping, Amir kept adding more and more items to the cart. I watched him, feeling his infectious excitement wash over me. *I love seeing this side of him.* When we finally reached the checkout counter, I glanced at the overflowing cart and realized how much we'd picked out. The cashier began ringing up the items, and the total quickly climbed.

"Your total is two thousand one hundred and sixty-seven dollars and fifty cents," the cashier announced, looking at us with a bright smile.

I turned to him. My eyes popped wide. "Wow, you went all out."

He shrugged with an unapologetic grin on his face. "I couldn't help myself."

And I couldn't bring myself to stop him. Seeing how happy he was and knowing he was doing it out of love for our baby made my heart swell with joy.

"Well, our baby is going to be the best-dressed kid around," I announced, giving him a playful nudge with my elbow.

He laughed while handing over his card to pay. "Only the best for our baby."

We left the store, bags in hand. The day had been so perfect that I almost forgot why I'd left him in the first place. But there was one question in the back of my mind that I couldn't shake.

"Were you serious about being done with your ex-fiancée?" I questioned, my voice laced with uncertainty.

He looked at me, his expression sincere. "Yeah. I am."

"What made you make the final decision? I hope you didn't do it because of me," I added quickly.

"It wasn't *all* you," he replied. "She wanted me to cut you completely out of my life and have us raise the baby together."

My eyebrows shot up in surprise. "Excuse me?"

"I told her she was crazy for saying that shit," he continued. "After she threw the engagement ring at my head, I got up outta there."

"Wow," I said, processing his words. "She sounds like a piece of work."

"That's putting it mildly. Remember the night I called you and told you things were officially over? That's when all that happened."

"I'm sorry I didn't want to hear you out," I admitted, feeling guilty for being in my feelings.

Amir shook his head as a gentle smile formed on his face. "I forgive you. I just want to work on moving forward. The last thing I'm trying to do is stress you, Rizzy. I don't want our baby born into chaos."

Relief washed over me. "Thank you for being understanding," I said softly. "It, uh, it means a lot."

We continued walking, and I found myself enjoying the moment more than I initially anticipated. A sense of contentment bubbled up inside me, giving way to a feeling of hope. Maybe, if the right stars aligned, Amir and I could navigate our parenthood journey together after all.

Amir

I was in the warehouse going over the inventory for the next shipment, when my phone buzzed with an incoming FaceTime call from Nerissa. Seeing her name on the screen, I quickly stepped outside to take the call. As soon as the call connected, I saw her face. She was visibly upset, with tears streaming down her warm brown cheeks.

"Nerissa, what's wrong?" I asked, my voice laced with concern.

She took a shaky breath before speaking. "I just left the doctor's office. She said my pregnancy is now considered high-risk. I have to be on pelvic rest for the remainder of my pregnancy," she announced before sobbing.

My heart sprinted up to my throat after hearing her words. "Oh my God, Rizzy. Is the baby okay? How did you even find this out? They said everything was okay at your last appointment a few weeks ago."

"I'd been experiencing some bright red spotting. I got concerned and called to make an appointment."

My brows lurched to my crisp hairline. "Spotting? For how long? Why the hell didn't you tell me, Nerissa?"

She sighed. "I'm sorry. I didn't think it would be anything more than first-time mother paranoia. I thought, '*Why worry him if everything could be fine?*'" she confessed.

"What happened when you went to the doctor?"

"She decided to run some tests to ensure everything was progressing smoothly with the baby. Then she called a couple of days ago and said she noticed some indicators in my test results that suggested my pregnancy might be at a higher risk, which prompted more tests and a thorough ultrasound yesterday morning."

I gripped the phone tighter, trying to mind my tone and not bite her head off for not including me when shit was going down at the moment.

"What exactly did she say to you when she called?" I probed.

"She sat me down and explained the situation. She said I have something called placenta previa."

"What the hell is that?"

"It means my placenta is covering some of my uterus."

"Does being high-risk mean you'll have a difficult pregnancy?"

She wagged her head. "Doctor Reed said it didn't. But we did talk about the need for me to be on pelvic rest to minimize any complications. I'm almost halfway through my pregnancy, and this is just not how I envisioned my last trimester going," she said, wiping away a tear.

"I know you're feeling overwhelmed right now, but everything will be okay. I promise you, we'll get through this together," I assured her.

She nodded while wiping away more tears. "I'm just so fucking scared right now, Amir. I don't know how I'm going to keep it together."

"You don't have to do it alone. I'm right here. Whatever you need, I'll provide. Do you want me to come over and keep you company? Or bring you anything?"

She shook her head, trying to muster up a small smile. "No, it's okay. I just needed to tell you. I'm going to cancel my clients for the rest of the day. I think I need some time to process everything."

I dipped my chin, accepting her wishes. "Okay," I said gently. "But I'm just a call away. I'll check in on you later, all right?"

"Okay," she replied, her voice softening. "Thanks, Amir."

"Take care of yourself," I said before flashing her a reassuring smile. "I'll talk to you later."

As we ended the FaceTime call, a surge of emotions took over my composure. The news of Nerissa's high-risk pregnancy hit me like a ton of fucking bricks. I was worried for her and our baby. I didn't even fully know what the fuck pelvic rest was, but the thought of her having to be on it for the next few months made me anxious as a mothafucka.

Beneath my worry was a nagging sense of helplessness that I couldn't shake. Despite all my reassurances to her that everything would be okay, I wasn't a doctor, and I damn sure didn't have a crystal ball to see into the future. I hated knowing there was only so much I could do. The health of our innocent baby and Nerissa's well-being was out of my control, and the weight of that uncertainty was heavier than the sands of the sea.

I knew I needed to step up and provide whatever support she needed, both emotionally and physically. I had her if she needed her groceries carried to her apartment and put away. If she needed her scalp washed and oiled, I was on it. If she needed me to rub her feet, cook her dinner, or drink her fucking bath water, I'd do it with no questions asked. That was how badly I fucked with her. The idea of her going through a high-risk pregnancy alone would never be her reality if it were up to me. I was determined to be there for her, to make sure she felt cared for and supported every day leading up to the delivery of our child.

Before returning to the warehouse, I made a mental note to check in on her every couple of hours and to start planning how I could help make the rest of her pregnancy as comfortable and stress-free as possible. I meant every fucking word I said to her. Whatever Nerissa needed, I was willing to provide.

I ENTERED THE BARBERSHOP AFTER HOURS, AND XL GAVE ME A nod while giving Ahsan a fresh cut. I quickly dapped them both up, still trying to steady my emotions before we settled down to talk business. I had to focus, even though my mind was still stuck on Nerissa and the baby.

"Any news on Demario?" I asked, speaking freely over the whirring of the clippers.

XL grunted. "We've been using Jules to keep tabs on his whereabouts. Turns out, getting her to flip on him was easy once his ass ghosted her. She said he caught a flight to Dallas but didn't know when or if he'd return to the city. We've been tapping her phone and have guards hidden in plain sight outside her apartment, keeping watch for that nigga."

I nodded, absorbing the information before I verbalized my thoughts. "Put a bounty on that nigga's head. I'll give one hundred thousand dollars to any nigga who can bring him to me alive. That way, whenever his ass does show up in Vegas again, the whole fuckin' city will be ready to handle him."

Ahsan dipped his chin. "Bet. That'll make sure this shit doesn't happen again."

XL put down the clippers and picked up his phone. "I'll get the word out." I watched him tap away at the screen in silence before two words slipped out of his mouth. "Oh shit."

"What?" I asked.

XL leaned in with a serious expression as he showed Ahsan the phone screen. "Somebody just sent me this," he said. "They spotted Rico in Miami."

My heart stuttered a frantic beat at the mention of Rico, the traitor who I suspected tried to take my brother's life. "Are you fucking serious?" I asked, my voice heavy with tension.

"It's that nigga. I'm sure of it," Ahsan confirmed before passing the phone to me.

I looked down at the screen. My jaw tightened as I studied the post from Rico's social media account from two days ago with the timestamp and location. "Stupid ass nigga."

"All right, we need to act fast," Ahsan stated.

"XL, I want you to take a couple of hittas and head to Miami to find that nigga. When you have confirmation about where he is, I want you to wait until I tell you to round that bitch ass nigga up and bring him back to Vegas. He needs to face judgment for what he fucking did. I'll make sure of that."

XL nodded, understanding the gravity of the situation. "Say less. I'll head out immediately. We'll get that mothafucka."

The unexpected news about Rico brought back memories and triggered a burning desire for vengeance. My blood boiled. I couldn't wait to put a bullet in that nigga's dome, but I had to stay focused and balanced, especially with everything going on with Nerissa's health and the baby.

I sighed heavily before changing the subject. "Yo, Nerissa called earlier and told me her pregnancy is high-risk. If I wasn't scared before, I'm scared as hell now."

Ahsan lowered his head. "Damn, that's tough. But it just means you need to be there for her even more and show her how committed you are and how much you care."

XL nodded in agreement. "Exactly. This is your chance to step up, lil nigga. Big Mama always said that adversity brought out the best in us. You've got her resilience, and you've got us too."

I sighed. "I don't know if I'm ready for this. Being a father... it's a lot. I'm scared I'll fuck it up. There's too much to lose now. I'm finally getting back in Nerissa's good graces, and I don't want to ruin things between us for life."

XL removed the cape and Ahsan got up out of the chair and came to sit beside me. "Yeah, it's a big responsibility. But you've taken on big shit before. And think about all the times Big Mama always used to tell us that family was everything. You've already got that shit embedded deep in your heart."

My cousin chimed in while he swept up around his booth. "Big Mama believed in us, and she believed in you. You just need to start believing in yourself, and you'll be straight. Fatherhood will suit you well."

I looked down before taking a deep breath. "I know, but what if I can't live up to all that shit? What if I fail her again?"

Ahsan put his hand on my shoulder. "You've got us, and she's got you. She saw enough good in you to want to have your baby, nigga. She could've handled it and said nothing to you, but that's not how it went because that's not how it was supposed to go. Just take shit one day at a time. You've got this."

"Thanks, yo. I needed to hear that."

Ahsan extended his fist to dap me up. "To family."

I smiled while bumping my fist against his. "To family."

Nerissa

J amia, one of my former colleagues, was in town on an overnight flight and contacted me to catch up. We were seated at a corner table, enjoying an early dinner together. The vibe was lively as we leaned in, done with our meals, and knee-deep in our conversation.

"Damn, girl! I'm so glad I got to catch up with you, Nerissa. I can't believe how much has changed since our last flight together!"

I chuckled while looking down at my growing belly. "I know, right? I'm so glad you're here. A hell of a lot has happened, and I've been feeling so overwhelmed lately."

"Why? What's going on?"

I sighed. "The doctor said I have a high-risk pregnancy, and I need to be on pelvic rest for the rest of it."

"Pelvic rest? Does that mean—"

"No fucking. No penetration. No orgasms. I feel so... worthless."

Jamia reached across the table, taking my hand with a reassuring grip. "Hey, now. You're anything but worthless. You're bringing a new life into this world. That's nothing to glaze over."

"Yeah, but I want to fuck!" I whined.

Jamia chuckled. "As much as it sucks, try to bench your worries for the next few months, all right? After you drop that baby, you'll be back to climbing the walls in no time."

"I just hate feeling like a burden."

"Has someone called you that?"

"No, but—"

"Okay, then. That's because you're not! This is totally out of your control and not your fault. Right now, you're doing what you gotta do to take care of yourself and your baby. That's the most important thing right now, period. It's okay to ask for help and lean on others occasionally so you don't overwhelm yourself. You're going to get through this."

I nodded, feeling a sliver of optimism. "Thanks, Jamia. I needed to hear that."

"Anytime, girl. So, what have you been up to since you decided to take a break from flying? Can you still do hair?" she asked, changing the subject to a lighter note.

"Yeah. I can still do all my normal day-to-day activities, so I've been doing hair full-time out of my apartment. It's been good. I love the flexibility it gives me, especially now with the baby on the way."

Her eyebrows shot up as she smiled. "That's wassup! Remind me to let you hook my edges up before my flight in the morning, okay? I can't get the baby hair swoop down to save my life!" she confessed with a chuckle.

I laughed alongside her. "I got you, girl."

"I always knew you had a talent for doing hair. How's business going now that you're local? I know you gained a lot of clients by traveling."

"It's different, but I've built up a good client base, and it's been great to finally put one hundred percent effort into doing something I'm passionate about."

"Yassss! I'm so happy for you, queen! It's great to see you thriving, not to mention that baby has got your pretty ass glowing!"

Our waiter approached us with a smile. "Sorry to interrupt,

ladies. I just wanted to let you know that your bill has been taken care of."

My brows dipped low. "What? By who?"

I'd heard of drive-through Samaritans who'd pay for the person's meal behind them, but never a stranger paying for a random ass meal.

"I'm not at liberty to say, but it's all covered. You two enjoy the rest of your evening."

I was confused but grateful, nonetheless. "Wow, okay. Thanks. You too."

Just as the waiter left, my phone vibrated against the table. I saw Amir's name on the screen and answered.

"Hey, can I call you back? I told you earlier I was going out to dinner at Juliano's Bistro with a friend," I said softly into the receiver.

"Hey. It's cool. I hope you two are having a good time."

"Yeah. We are. Someone just randomly paid for our entire meal."

"It was me," he confessed.

"What?"

"Don't freak out, but I wanted to do something nice for you, so I called the restaurant and took care of the bill."

"Amir, are you serious right now?"

"Yes, I'm serious. I just wanted to do something to show you I care, even when I'm not around."

His words made my heart soften even more than it already was. *That was so unexpected and sweet.* Amir had been so attentive and sweet since I told him my pregnancy was considered high-risk. He tried to be there for me and the baby as much as I'd allow. He hired a cleaning lady to come into my apartment weekly to tidy up, wash dishes and clothes, and do whatever light housework I needed. Per my doctor's orders, he allowed me to drive only on short trips. Anything over twenty minutes, he made sure to drive me himself or ensure I had rideshare service. Part of me was grateful for his support, especially since Demario was like a ghost in the wind. It felt good to have someone care so much. But another part of me was afraid of getting hurt again, dreading the day he'd wake up and revert to his old, childish ways.

"Wow. I don't know what to say other than thank you."

"Say less. You deserve it. Get back to your friend. I'll talk to you later."

A smile crawled up my face. "Bye, Amir."

Despite the fear gnawing at my gut, I couldn't fight the spark of love I still held for him deep down. Amir's actions were slowly breaking down the walls I'd built around my heart, making me secretly consider a future together. I still needed to protect my peace for myself and my baby, but his genuine efforts were making it damn hard to keep my guard up.

I hung up and traded glances with Jamia, who was watching her with a curious expression.

She arched a questioning brow. "Was that *him?*"

I nodded. "Yeah. It was. He was the one who paid for our meals."

"Seriously? Last time I checked, you were trying to get over him, and now you're pregnant. So, what's going on with you two now that there's a baby involved?"

I sighed, conflicted. "It's still complicated as hell, girl. If I'm being one hundred percent honest with myself, I know I still have feelings for him, but I'm petrified to let my fucking guard down. He's done some shit in the past that makes it hard to trust him completely."

She nodded. "Trust me, I get it. Ain't nothing worse than a woman with a scorned heart, but I mean, randomly paying for our meals was thoughtful of him."

"Yeah, it caught me off guard too. It's not like him to do something like this. But it's like, ever since I told him about the baby and that my pregnancy was high-risk, he's been going above and beyond for me whenever I let him."

"Damn, girl. It sounds like he's making an effort and cares about you. You've been thinking about giving him another chance, haven't you?"

"I have, but it's just hard to know what to believe sometimes. It's like I'm always waiting for the other shoe to drop with him."

"I get it. But actions speak louder than words, right? And today's action was a good sign, Nerissa. Don't overlook that."

"You're right. I need to figure out what will be best for me and the baby in the long run."

"We both know you know what's best for you and the baby. Now it's time to figure out what's best for your heart."

A FEW MINUTES AFTER DINNER WITH JAMIA, I FOUND MYSELF sitting in the driver's seat of my car with my phone in hand. I hadn't been able to get Amir off my mind since our conversation about him. I took a deep breath, resting one hand on my stomach while the other dialed Amir's number and waited as it rang.

"Nerissa, Wassup?"

"H-hey, Amir," I stammered. "Are you busy? There's something I need to get off my chest. Can I come over?"

"Is everything okay? You sound serious," he replied, sounding concerned.

My chest deflated with a hard sigh. "Yeah, everything's fine. I just need to talk to you in person."

"All right. I'm texting you the address and room number of the hotel I'm staying at. Let me know how far away it is from where you are."

"Okay, thanks," I said, while copying the address into my GPS. "It's only eleven miles away, and a twenty-three minute drive. I'll be there soon."

"No you won't. It's over twenty minutes. Leave your car. I'll come to you."

"Relax, Amir. It's only a few more minutes over my limit. I promise I'll be fine. And once I'm in your care, I'll let you drive me or my car wherever, okay?"

"Fine. Take your time, Rizzy. I'll be here."

I hung up as my mind raced with thoughts of everything I needed to get off my chest regarding how I felt about Amir Patton.

I STOOD OUTSIDE AMIR'S HOTEL ROOM, MY HEART THUMPING like a bucking bronco as I knocked on the door. He opened it, looking surprised and pleased to see me standing there.

He greeted me with a handsome grin. "Come in."

"Thanks."

I stepped inside, looking around as the door closed behind me. His spacious hotel suite proved Amir had a taste for the finer things in life. I followed him into the living area, where a plush, oversized blue velvet sofa sat before a glass coffee table. A large, flat-screen TV was secured to the center of the wall, and the sheer curtains in front of the floor-to-ceiling windows highlighted the view of the Vegas Strip.

The kitchenette was equipped with top-of-the-line stainless steel appliances and marble countertops. Nearby was a small dining area, perfect for two, with a crystal chandelier hanging overhead. The open layout provided a straight sight line from the living area to the king-sized bed on the other side of the suite with a luxurious, tufted, blue velvet headboard and crisp white linens.

"This place is nice, but why are you staying in a hotel?" I quizzed before getting to the real reason I'd shown up.

He sighed. "I'm making arrangements to have my things removed from the apartment I shared with my ex, so for now, it's hotel living."

"What made you propose to her in the first place?" I asked curiously.

He paused before speaking up. "I thought it would make me grow up. I wanted my brother to see me as a man, not the same childish ass kid he damn near helped raise. Plus, I was turning thirty. I kept asking myself how long I could keep playing around. I was in the mall, saw the ring, and spontaneously bought that shit. I never even planned to ask her right away, but she found the ring hidden in the back of the closet and asked me about it. I had to come clean. Then she went on about how she wanted a fairytale proposal, so that's when I asked her to marry me at my birthday party."

My brows heightened as we sat down on the couch. "So, wait. It was all staged?"

Amir dipped his chin. "Yeah. She wanted a show, and I gave her one. But now I know better. If fucking with Brandi taught me anything, it was that real ass relationships aren't about expensive ass grand gestures or putting on a show for niggas on social media to talk about. They're about being honest and sincere."

"Wow."

"Are you surprised?"

"I mean, yeah. Kind of. I never thought I'd see the day you'd take accountability for your actions. I have to say, I'm impressed."

"You wanna know the craziest thing about it?"

"What?"

"I never told a soul about that shit until now."

"Really?"

"Yeah. But why'd you want to come here to talk? What's on your mind?"

I took a deep breath. "I'm here because I feel like we're inching closer to my due date, and I need to be honest with you. And the truth is, I've been feeling torn about us for a while now."

"Torn, how?"

"On the one hand, I still have feelings for you, but on the other, I'm scared as hell to give you the chance to hurt me again."

"I know I was the one who fucked things up between us, so I don't blame you for feeling that way. I know it's hard to trust me. But I'm here now and willing to do whatever it takes to make things right between us, Nerissa. I put that on my Big Mama."

My vision blurred with tears. "It's just so damn hard. I wanna trust you, but there's this nagging feeling that you're going to let me down."

"I have the same feeling."

"You do? Why?"

"Because I know it's my job to show you how important you are to me. I wasted my chance with you back then, but I don't want to make the same mistakes twice. I've been walking on eggshells around you ever since I found out you were pregnant, trying not to fuck things up. I'm not asking you to trust me overnight. I'm just asking that you allow me to show you all the ways I want to do right by you and our baby."

I huffed as I looked down. "It's just hard because the nicer you are to me, the harder it gets to stop myself from falling for you again. I'm all over the place with how to feel. One minute, I'm angry at you and ready to rip your fucking head off your shoulders, and the next, you do something unexpectedly sweet like paying for my food, and it confuses me!"

Amir gently lifted my chin. "I understand. But we can take it slow—one step at a time. No pressure. Whatever you decide, I'll be here."

I shot him a half smile, feeling more at ease, knowing he would take things slow and be there for me.

"Okay."

"You got anything else you need to get off your chest?"

"That's all for right now."

"How'd things go with your friend?"

"It was good seeing her and catching up. I miss flying, but I'm glad to be doing hair full-time."

He smirked. "You know, I still have this expired version of you in my head. I'm sure you've changed, and I want to know the version of you now."

"Well, yeah. A lot has changed, even besides the baby. I feel like I've found my passion for doing hair. Since moving back here, I've been working out of my apartment, and it's been amazing. I love making women feel good about themselves."

He nodded. "That's wassup. I had no idea."

"But with the baby coming, I know I won't be able to travel as freely. So, I have this crazy ass goal of opening my own shop one day. I don't even care if it's in the basement of my damn house, y'know? I just want something of my own. It's a big dream, but I don't know. I think I can make it happen."

Amir smirked. "That's wassup. I'm proud of you."

"Thanks, Amir."

"Hey, uh, you got anything to do for the next few hours?" he asked, resting his hand against his nape.

"No. Why?"

"Well, since you're here, how about I buy your favorite ice cream, and we just kick it for a bit like old times? Again, no pressure and no expectations."

I sighed. "Fine. But only because you mentioned ice cream, and I've been craving some cookies and cream."

He grabbed the room phone to order the ice cream through room service. "You want me to see if they got some bacon too?"

My eyes lit up. "Oh my God, yes!"

"I got you."

Amir

Nerissa and I were sitting on the sofa in my hotel suite, eating ice cream and scrolling through movie options on the TV. The energy between us was more relaxed than it had been in a long time.

She cleared her throat before putting her spoon down in her bowl and turning her attention to me. "I'm probably going to regret asking you this, but I wanna know the answer too damn bad..."

"What is it?" I asked curiously.

"Why'd you cheat on me when we were together, Amir? I thought we had something good."

I swallowed hard, looking down, knowing the day would come when I'd have to face judgment for the shit I did in my past. I paused, gathering my words, knowing she wouldn't accept anything but honesty.

"There's no excuse for what I did. We both know I fucked up. But the truth is, I was scared. Scared of how real things were getting between us. Scared about how I felt about you when I knew I wasn't ready to be the nigga you needed me to be. So, I did something fucking stupid and selfish."

"But what was so special about her? She must've had something I didn't or gave you something I couldn't."

I shook my head, unable to remember the broad's name, let alone the details of her features. "That ho is just as unimportant to me now as she was then, Nerissa. It was never about her. It was about me running away from a good thing because of my insecurities," I admitted. "I thought I could escape everything by fucking around with someone else, but all I did was hurt you and ruin the best relationship I've ever had."

A tear slipped down her cheek, and she quickly turned her head away. "There was a time when I loved you with my whole heart, Amir. You're right, we *did* have something good, and you balled it up and threw it away. I never really got over that."

I reached out to hold her hand. "I know. And I'm sorry. I never regretted it more than after seeing you again on that plane and seeing the pain still there, knowing I caused it. I regret that shit every single day, Rizzy. You and I had something I've never been able to copy and paste with another female. I was made to be *your* nigga, Nerissa. I know I can't change the past, but I'm willing to do whatever it takes to earn back your trust and show you I can be the man you deserve."

She smiled gently through her tears. "Okay."

"Can I ask you something I might regret now?"

She shrugged. "Go for it."

"Did you ever consider... *not* keeping the baby once you found out? I mean, considering how much you hated me for what I did to you."

"No," she replied, her voice firm.

"Forreal? Because I wouldn't blame you if you did."

"There was never a question whether or not I was going to keep my baby, Amir, whether you were around or not. How I look at it is God blessed me with this baby. He chose me. You could've procreated with anyone, and it turned out to be me."

"And I'm grateful every day for it."

"Seriously?"

"Hell yeah. My last relationship was a goddamn nightmare, Rizzy. Like, forreal."

"That's karma for your ass."

I tossed up my hands in surrender. "Makes sense. She brought out the absolute worst in a nigga. I'm glad that chapter of my life is over."

"Two years ago, you couldn't have paid me a million bucks to believe I'd be writing this chapter of my life with you someday. I *never* planned to rewrite our story."

"Is that what we're doing, Rizzy? Rewriting?"

"Maybe," she answered before gasping and placing her hand on her belly. "Oh shit, the baby just kicked. Do you want to feel it?"

My eyes popped wide. "Really? Hell yeah, I'd love to."

Nerissa took my hand and gently placed it on her round belly. We waited for a moment, and then the baby kicked again. My face lit up with shock and joy. "Oh shit! Wow! That feels crazy!"

"Pretty incredible, right?"

"I can't believe it," I responded with a grin.

Caught up in the moment, I leaned in and kissed Nerissa. I pulled back almost immediately, realizing what I'd done. I'd been preaching all night about taking shit one step at a time, and there I was, already trying to go to first base.

"Shit, I'm sorry, Rizzy. I didn't mean to…"

She cut me off. "Don't apologize, Amir."

She leaned in and kissed me back, that time with more certainty that I had her permission. The kiss was tender and filled with unspoken words and feelings. We pulled away after a few seconds, both a little breathless.

It had been a long time since I'd felt so close to her. Kissing Nerissa felt like coming home, like a piece of my heart that had been missing for the last couple of years was finally back in its rightful place. I'd missed her like people in the desert missed the rain. So much more than I initially realized. Maybe there was still a chance we'd find our way back to each other when everything was said and done.

Nerissa sighed heavily, the frustration evident in her eyes. "I hate feeling so helpless," she admitted, her voice trembling. "Not being able to... *feel* you is driving me crazy."

I gently massaged her scalp, offering a comforting touch. "I know it's a tough stretch, but you're doing everything you need to do to make sure you and our child are safe. I don't give a fuck about pussy. I'm not going to shrivel up and die without it. All that matters to me is your safety. You could never be a burden to me."

Whatever was happening to her wasn't her fault. She was putting her body through hell to give me a child. I couldn't take that for granted.

She looked up at me with tears glistening in her eyes. "I just feel so damn useless, fat, and ugly."

I shook my head. "Nah. You're far from useless, and you're gorgeous. You don't see what I see."

"What do you see when you look at me, Amir?"

"I see a woman that's strong and feisty, a woman that don't take shit from nobody. I see a woman who refuses to be defeated no matter what curveballs life throws her way. I see you, Rizzy. And this right here, this is just a temporary phase, all right? And I'm right here to help you through it. Besides, I'm up for the challenge of finding other ways to get you off. You should know by now that I love your dirty drawers, Rizzy."

She sucked her teeth. "Ew, Amir, that's nasty."

I chuckled. "So what? I'm a nasty ass nigga. You know you like it."

She giggled. "Whatever."

I smirked as I pulled her closer, enveloping her in my arms. "I like how you say my name, even when you're mad or annoyed."

She leaned into my touch. "Just be lucky you have a name I've never not liked saying," she whispered.

"Now take off your clothes," I instructed.

"W-what?"

"You heard me, Rizzy. Strip or I'll do it for you."

After peeling off every article of clothing on her body, she followed me over to the bed. I grabbed a bottle of baby oil gel and pulled my shirt over my head before joining her on the bed. She lay down, surrounded by pillows, as I massaged her entire body from head to toe.

I completed her full body massage and took off the rest of my clothes before lying between her legs. Nerissa ran her slim fingers through my waves and lightly scratched my back while we lay naked, doing skin-to-skin. The movie on the TV played in the background as we took turns rubbing and touching each other underneath the covers as if we'd been transported back in time to high school. It was the most intimate, sensual experience I'd ever had without bussing a nut. It felt good to know we could expand our relationship beyond sex and still feel just as connected.

LATER THE FOLLOWING WEEK, I CONVINCED NERISSA TO GO ON A double date with Ahsan and Sienna. Their wedding day was approaching, and I didn't want their special day to be the first time I made introductions. The restaurant was lively, and the vibe between the four of us was positive, unlike the last double date I'd experienced.

I grinned. "Yo, I'm so glad we could all get together tonight. It's been a while since we've had a night out like this."

Ahsan nodded. "For sure. It's great to see you smiling so damn much. Happiness looks good on you, bruh."

"Thanks," I said before gesturing toward Nerissa. "Ahsan, this is Nerissa. I don't know if you remember her when we were together."

He smiled. "I think I vaguely remember meeting you once or twice."

"Don't feel bad. Two years is a long time. It's good to see you again."

Ahsan then directed his attention to his girl. "And this is my fiancée, Sienna."

Sienna eyed her closely before smiling politely. "Hi... I'm sorry, but have we met before? You look kind of familiar."

Nerissa shook her head. "No, I don't think so. Unless maybe it was thirty thousand feet in the air. I used to be a flight attendant."

"No, that's not it."

"I also do hair. If not that, I'm not sure where we might have met then."

Sienna shook her head as if letting it all brush off her shoulders. "It's probably nothing. Anyway, it's nice to meet you. And you're glowing, might I add," she complimented. "Pregnancy looks good on you."

"Thanks. You look radiant yourself. And congrats on the upcoming wedding. I'm happy for you both. This must be such an exciting time for you two."

"I don't know if exciting is the word, but we're hanging in there," Sienna said.

Before we were seated, I leaned over to Ahsan and handed him my phone. "Hey, can you get a picture of us?"

"Of course."

He took my phone and snapped a few pictures of the two of us before handing it back. I looked through the photos. We were smiling and looking happy with our hands on her round belly.

I turned the phone to Nerissa to show her the best one. "This one is perfect. Do you mind if I post it?"

Nerissa shook her head. "You're lucky I look cute in that one, so it's cool. Go ahead."

I posted the photo with the caption: *Feeling incredibly blessed to have the opportunity to be on this parenthood journey with @Nerissa-Barnes. I'm excited to announce that we're expecting a little one soon! #Blessed #Family #NewBeginnings*

Our mini photo shoot immediately prompted Sienna to ask Nerissa about the pregnancy, showing genuine interest.

"So, do you two know if it's a boy or a girl yet?"

"No. We're waiting to find out the sex," Nerissa announced.

"Any predictions on what you think it is?" Ahsan quizzed, hopping into the conversation.

Nerissa rubbed her belly. "I don't know. Sometimes, I think it's a boy. Other days, I'm almost certain it's a girl."

Once seated, Ahsan took over the conversation while we waited for our drinks.

"So, I've got some exciting news about my land development project. The grand opening for the first building is scheduled a couple of weeks before the wedding."

I laughed. "Nigga, you're a madman. Aligning two big things so close together like that? You're asking for trouble."

Sienna nodded in agreement. "That's what I've been trying to tell him, but you know your brother is as hardheaded as they come. Weddings are stressful enough. He better be lucky I'm not a bridezilla!"

Nerissa laughed. "That sounds like a lot to handle. How are you two managing everything? How far away is the wedding day?"

"Fifty days and counting," Sienna announced.

"Oh, wow! I bet that feels like tomorrow for you, huh?"

"Exactly!"

"That's how I feel about my due date. Pregnancy has been challenging, but I'm excited to meet our little one."

Ahsan nodded. "I can't wait to be an uncle."

"When are you two gonna come around with a bun in the oven so our little one can have someone to play with?" I inquired.

"Damn, Amir! One thing at a time. Can I get this man down the aisle first?" Sienna answered with a soft chuckle.

I snickered. "Trust me, with the way I know he feels about you, that nigga will be there with bells on."

"I know you are not trying to sit across this table and call me whipped like you not over there looking like Cool Whip your damn self," Ahsan jabbed.

The four of us laughed before I changed the subject. "But seriously, how's the development project coming along?"

"It's coming along great. We had a few hurdles initially, but I can see the finish line, at least the first of many."

Sienna cheesed. "Yeah. I'm proud of my bae."

I pulled my attention away from the conversation to check my phone. Not even fifteen minutes after I posted about the baby, my phone started blowing up with texts and notifications. Among them was a comment from Brandi underneath the photo.

Brandi: *Wow. Really Amir? Didn't realize you were such a "family man" now. Guess some niggas really can change overnight. Best of luck to you and your break baby. Bet you thought you got one up on me. Your last name sounded ugly with my first name anyway! #FuckYourNewBeginnings."*

Her comment dripped with sarcasm and jealousy, aimed at making everything about my character look insincere. All her miserable ass wanted to do was stir up drama and make the niggas on the internet question my authenticity.

I sucked my teeth. "This *bitch.*"

"What is it?" Ahsan asked, sensing the shift in my mood.

"Brandi is talking shit under my post about the baby."

"What? What exactly did she say?" Nerissa asked. I handed over my phone to her so she could read the comment. She frowned. "Wow. Seriously?"

"Misery loves company, y'all. Don't even let her get to you. Just block her and move on, Amir."

I nodded while swiping from my social media feeds to my unread DMs and texts. After reading messages from people in my circle, including some of Brandi's "day ones," she told people we were still together. She wasn't wearing her ring because I was getting it resized and adding more diamonds to it. It was one lie after another. The announcement about my unborn child was proof that I'd moved on and had her looking like a straight-up clown.

"Sienna's right," Ahsan interjected. "Don't breathe any more life into that toxic ass situation."

I shook my head, torn between my emotions and my logic. On the one hand, I wanted to clear my name and tell everyone who the true liar was. On the other, I had chosen to be done with Brandi for a reason. Going back and feeding into her negative energy just felt like a trap.

My head swiveled in Nerissa's direction. "Can I handle this real quick? She won't stop until I put her in her place. I just don't want you thinking I'm on no bullshit."

"Better you than me. Go handle your business, Amir," Nerissa responded, giving me the permission I sought.

I stepped away from the table for a moment to call Brandi. She picked up on the third ring, just like I knew her ass would. She'd been awaiting my call ever since she'd left that nasty ass comment underneath my post.

"Why the fuck are you calling my phone, nigga?" Brandi snapped, choosing violence.

"Listen, B. You need to stop with the fucking lies, all right? We're not together anymore, and you know that! You ain't getting the ring back. I've got the movers handling my shit. We're done! I've moved on, and your miserable ass should too."

"How the fuck could you do this shit to me, Amir? After all the shit I put up with from you? You know that post made me look like a fucking fool!"

"Like I said, it's time to move the fuck on. Nerissa is back in my life, and we're having a baby. Respect that shit."

"Fuck you and your respect, nigga! I'll be damned if I'll be happy about you having a baby on me with some washed-up bitch from your past!"

My jaw tightened as I gripped the phone tighter. Had we been face-to-face, I probably would've snapped her neck for talking crazy about Nerissa like that. "I don't know what alternate fuckin' universe you live in, but I didn't have a baby on you, Brandi. We talked about it! When things went down between Nerissa and me, we were broken up! So I don't give a fuck if you're happy about it or not. Just stop spreading lies, bitch. Now delete my number!" I growled.

I hung up and returned to the table, relieved that I'd chosen to clear the air and show my unwavering commitment to Nerissa and the baby. I traded glances with my brother before looking at Nerissa. She watched me with concern in her expression.

"You good?"

"Yeah. I told her ass to stop with the lies and move the fuck on. I'm not letting shit come between me being able to raise our child together, and that's on Big Mama."

Nerissa smiled. "Thank you for handling that. I appreciate your honesty."

I laced my hand with hers underneath the table. "Always."

"Now that that's over, let's get back to enjoying our evening, shall we?" Sienna added.

Nerissa

After we ate, I stood to excuse myself. "I need to use the ladies' room. I'll be right back."

Sienna nodded. "Wait up. I'll join you."

As we walked to the restroom, Sienna scrolled through her phone while I made a B-line for the nearest private stall. After relieving myself, I exited the spacious stall and saw her standing at the sink with her arms folded across her chest.

"I saw Amir's social media post. I didn't know your last name was Barnes."

I dipped my chin while running my soapy hands under the stainless steel faucet. "Yeah. It is."

Sienna hesitated. "You wouldn't happen to have a brother, would you?"

I nodded while snatching a few pieces of paper towel to dry my hands. "I do. His name is Demario."

All the color left Sienna's face, and she looked visibly shaken.

My brows creased. "Are you okay, Sienna? Why did you react like that when I said his name?"

She drew in a quick breath before taking a step back. "Now I know where I know you from."

"What?"

"Listen, I don't want to stress you out, but Demario is my ex, and he's been causing problems for me, Ahsan, and Amir ever since his ass got out of prison. And now you show up out of the blue pregnant with Amir's child... It's just all hitting too close to home right now, and I'm trying hard not to freak the fuck out right now."

My chest tightened. "What? Oh my God. I–I had no idea. Demario and I are half-siblings. We didn't have a tight relationship when he went to prison. We didn't keep in touch like that. It was only recently we started to try and rebuild our relationship."

"Demario and I were only together briefly before he went to prison. It wasn't like he talked about you daily, but I remember him telling me he had a sister."

"Talk about a small fucking world."

"Does Amir know?"

I nodded. "He does."

She folded her arms across her chest. "Don't lie to me, Nerissa."

"Listen, I can see that this news has visibly upset you. I want you to know that I had no idea about your connection to my brother. If I had known, I would have told you sooner when you asked if we knew each other. And I swear Amir knows Demario is my brother."

"Do you know where he is now?" she probed, pressing me hard.

"No. I haven't been in contact with him for weeks. I don't want to be held accountable for his actions."

Sienna exhaled while leaning against the granite countertop. "It's just a lot to fucking process while I'm standing right here in your face. I don't think you understand how much shit Demario's been stirring up since he got out. I can't believe he's *your* brother..."

I nodded. "I understand. Yes, we're blood, but that doesn't mean I condone his actions. I'm truly sorry for whatever he put you through, but I want to focus on a drama-free future with Amir and our baby."

"I appreciate you saying that. It's just... Ahsan never mentioned any of this to me. So either that means Amir knows and hasn't said shit, or Ahsan hasn't been telling me the whole truth. And I don't like feeling like the nigga I'm about to marry is keeping me in the dark about shit."

I sighed. "If he knows, I don't know why Ahsan didn't tell you, but I can assure you that Amir knows."

"How did he find out?"

"It was a complete shit show the day I randomly ran into him while I was having lunch with my brother's girlfriend, Jules."

Sienna held out her hand to stop me. "I'm sorry. *Who?*"

"Yeah. I know. Amir followed me back to our table, and as soon as she saw him, it was like she'd seen a ghost. I didn't know the girl could run that damn fast. That's when Amir told me she used to work for his brother."

"That obsessed ass bitch is a basket case, but that's a story for another day. Continue."

"Amir had me pull up a picture of my brother, and as soon as I did, he linked him to whatever shit he's been dealing with. But I promise you, Sienna, I had no idea. The last thing I wanted to do was to move back to Vegas and fall into drama."

"All this shit sounds like one big fucking setup, and I don't like it," Sienna said, pacing from one end of the countertop to the other. "No. If Amir knows, then nine times out of ten, so does Ahsan, which means his ass never mentioned it to me on purpose. I can't believe he kept this shit from me!"

"Again, I'm sorry. I don't want my brother's actions to come between us when we're just getting to know each other."

Sienna stopped pacing long enough to turn her attention to me. "Thank you for being honest with me. Let's just see if I can get through the rest of the night without murdering my fiancé, and we'll figure out everything else from there."

Finding out Sienna was my brother's ex was the last thing I expected. I could tell she'd been through a lot because of him. My heart went out to her. I knew firsthand how difficult he could be. *No wonder she thought I looked so familiar. I wonder if this means she's the one whose cousin helped him rob her apartment.* I didn't know all the facts, and I didn't want to go around spewing misinformation. All I knew was that wherever my brother was, his ass needed to stay there if he knew what was good for him. Returning to Vegas would surely only seal his fate.

I wondered if Amir had told his brother about my relation to Demario. If he did, why didn't Ahsan mention it to Sienna? It was easy to see I was in a situation that could get even more complicated in the blink of an eye. The last thing I wanted was more stress, especially with the baby on the way. I wanted to protect my peace and hoped we could all move past it without either of us having to choose a side.

***

Two days later, I was sitting on the couch when my phone rang with a call from an unknown number. I quickly tapped ignore, not in the mood for a telemarketer's bullshit. The phone rang again and another time after that before I answered.

"Who the hell is this playing on my phone?" I barked into the receiver.

"Chill, sis. It's me, D. You alone?"

My heartbeat went haywire as I gripped the phone tighter. "Demario? What the hell? Where have you been? And yeah, I'm alone."

"I told you I had to lay low, but I'm back, and I need to pull up on you. You're about to get a text from me. Reply with your address."

"My address? Demario, are you seriously back in Vegas?" I asked just as my phone dinged with a text.

"Send me your address. I'll see you soon, all right?" he replied before ending the call.

I hesitated before opening the message and responding with my address. I was just glad Amir wasn't around. *What the fuck am I getting myself into?*

Half an hour later, there was a knock on my door. *Fuck. He's here.* I felt a wave of uncertainty wash over me as I opened the door to see Demario standing there. His presence brought back a flood of memories, both good and bad. I stepped to the side, a non-verbal invite inside, and we sat in my living room.

"Wow. Look at you," he said, eyeing my belly that had grown substantially since we'd last seen each other.

"Yeah."

"How's the pregnancy going?"

"It's going, Demario. Now cut the small talk, and let's handle it straight. Tell me why you're back in Vegas when we both know you shouldn't be," I stated, my voice tinged with suspicion.

"I saw your post."

"What post?"

"The one that bitch ass mothafucka tagged you in. Never thought you'd let a bitch nigga change up the way you move with your own family, but I guess I gotta stop expecting too much outta people."

I frowned, feeling my blood pressure elevate. "Excuse me? What are you even talking about right now?"

Demario leaned back, his eyes scanning the room before settling on me. "I need to know where your loyalty lies, Nerissa. You're pregnant by Amir, the brother of my enemy. How could you let this shit happen?"

My skin bristled at his accusatory tone. "You, of all people, don't get to question my fucking choices, Demario. *You* are the one who hasn't been around all these years! You don't know what I've been through! In fact, you don't know shit about me or my life!"

He sighed, rubbing his temples. "Your ass needs to understand why this is a big deal for me. Sienna... she was *everything* to me. While I was locked up, her cousin Zyon kept me updated about her, sent me money, y'know, made a nigga feel like I still had a connection to the outside world while doing my time. But when I got out, Sienna didn't want anything to do with me. She'd moved on with that nigga Ahsan."

A small part of my heart ached for my brother. I knew how it felt to not be with the one your heart yearned for. "I'm sorry, Demario. But what does that have to do with me and Amir?"

"Everything," he replied. "You're carrying this nigga's brother's child. It feels like every bit of betrayal."

I felt a lump in my throat. I was torn. I understood his pain but knew that my relationship with Amir was complicated. I hated that something so beautiful like love could get so dangerous. "I didn't know about any of this, and I'm not trying to get in the middle of your shit, Maree, but I need you to be careful. We both know it's not safe for you here."

"I'm only back for twenty-four hours to tie up some loose ends, and then I'm gone in the wind again. I just wanted to talk to you face to face and let you know what's up."

"So, does this mean you hate me now because of who my child's father is?"

He shook his head as he stood to leave. "We family. I can dislike your ass, but I could never hate you." He touched my stomach briefly before pulling me into a tight hug. "You take care of yourself, all right?"

I hugged him back. "You too."

No sooner than I closed the door and turned on my heel toward the living room, the sharp, ringing sound of multiple gunshots and the screeching of tires flooded my ears. My chest vibrated with my pounding heart as I raced toward the window to look outside my blinds. The moment I saw my brother sprawled out on the pavement, my pulse went jagged. Everything from that point on was a blur. There was a 9-1-1 call. I barely remember the sound of the operator's monotonous voice. There was an ambulance ride. And tears. Lots of fucking tears.

Amir

I trekked through the large, vacant home with my realtor, Sandra. The five-thousand square foot house was impressive, with five spacious bedrooms, four bathrooms, a gourmet kitchen, and a large backyard—a luxury we never had growing up.

Sandra smiled warmly at me, "So, Mr. Patton, does the property check all your boxes?"

I nodded without hesitation, a knowing smile on my face. "It does. It's time to start putting down real roots."

Just then, my phone rang. Excusing myself, I stepped away to take the call. I was surprised to hear one of my hittas on the other end informing me that Demario had been hit in a drive-by shooting and was en route to the hospital. My heart almost leaped straight out of my chest. My opp had been taken down, and I had *nothing* to do with it. XL was still in Miami, so I quickly tossed out the idea of the shooter being him or Rico.

"Is he dead?" I asked, voice low into the receiver.

"I don't know. He had a girl with him in the ambulance."

"Who?"

"I don't know. Some pregnant bitch."

I gripped the phone tighter, knowing he was referring to Nerissa. "Keep me posted," I growled before ending the call.

Still shocked, I quickly dialed my brother. Ahsan answered on the second ring.

"Yeah?"

"Where are you, nigga?"

"At the site. Why?"

"Did you hear?"

"Hear what?"

"Demario got shot up. He's on the way to the hospital," I said, my voice filled with disbelief.

He paused. "No, I hadn't heard. Is the nigga dead?" he quizzed, responding with more curiosity than remorse.

I sighed, processing the unexpected news. "I don't know. I was told Nerissa was with him in the ambulance. I'm about to try and track her down at the hospital."

"Hit me when you know something."

"Bet. We need to discuss our next steps."

As I hung up, I glanced back at the house, realizing that while I was ready to put down roots for my growing family, the world around me was still as cold and unpredictable as ever.

***

I ARRIVED AT THE EMERGENCY ROOM DOORS, MY HEART pounding with worry as I raced inside. My eyes hurriedly scanned the waiting room until I spotted Nerissa sitting in a corner, trembling with her brother's blood on her clothes. I raced over to her, my concern apparent.

"Nerissa, what happened?" I inquired, my voice filled with urgency.

She looked up at me, her red, puffy eyes filled with tears. "Why the fuck are you here right now?"

"What? Where else would I be besides right here for you?"

"How did you even know I was here, huh? You fucking spying on me?"

I paused, knowing I needed to choose my words carefully. I couldn't tell her I had hittas posted outside her apartment complex, watching and waiting for Demario to pop out of the dirt like a groundhog in February.

I reached out to her. "Rizzy, just tell me that you're okay."

She snatched her arm away. "Don't fucking touch me, Amir."

"All I'm trying to do is be here for you. Why won't you let me?"

"Because my skin crawls whenever I look at you!" she yelled.

I looked around us. Her tone had drawn the eyes of sick people and nurses alike. Everyone noticed the commotion.

She drove her index finger into my chest, drawing my attention back to her. "We both know you wanted him dead after what he stole from you. How do I know you didn't have anything to do with it? How do I know you weren't sitting outside waiting to pull the trigger?" she accused, her voice shaking with emotion.

My eyes widened in shock, although I knew she wasn't wrong. I did want that nigga dead. But I didn't kill him. "Nerissa, I swear to you, I had nothing to do with this. I swear," I pleaded, trying to reach out to her again.

But she pulled away, her face twisted with pain and worry. "I can't deal with seeing you right now. Just leave, Amir. Please," she begged, her voice breaking.

"You can say what you want. I'm not leaving you like this."

My refusal to listen to her only set her off more. "When are you going to stop lying to me, huh? I've seen the same cars near the entrance and exits of my apartment complex for weeks, Amir! I know you've been watching me! I was just waiting for you to say something."

I sighed. "*Yes.* I had someone watching your apartment and Jules's apartment for signs of Demario, but I promise you I *didn't* do this shit. I know he's your blood, and I've respected that. I wouldn't hurt you like that, Nerissa. I don't know how else to prove I didn't do it."

She cut her glossy eyes at me. "It doesn't matter what you say. I don't fucking believe you!"

Before I could respond, two guards with stern expressions approached us. *Fuck. One of the nurses must have called security.*

"Sir, we're going to have to ask you to leave," one of the guards said firmly.

My frustration boiled over the minute one of them put their fucking hands on my shoulder. I quickly jerked away. "Don't fucking touch me! I didn't do shit wrong!" I shouted, my fists clenched tight and ready to strike a mothafucka.

The guards moved closer, ready to escort my ass off the premises. "Sir, please cooperate. We're here to deescalate the situation. We don't want any trouble."

I glared at them, my anger barely contained. "If either one of you mothafuckas lay another hand on me, I promise you'll be sharing a room in this bitch," I warned.

Seeing the situation escalate further, one of the nurses stepped in. "Sir, please, for everyone's safety, just leave peacefully. This isn't helping anyone."

Realizing the truth in her firm but gentle tone, I took a deep breath, my tense shoulders sagging with hesitance. I looked back at Nerissa one last time, my heart heavy with regret. "Nerissa, I promise you, I had nothing to do with this," I said softly before turning and leaving the hospital.

Security remained only a half step away until I was at least fifty feet from the building. I got back to my car and slammed the door. I sighed. All that back and forth, and I still hadn't figured out if the nigga was still breathing.

Nerissa's words weighed heavily on me. We'd been doing so good, and things had been smoother than butter between us, but now that her brother had been shot, she'd chosen to put my name all over it without hearing me out. I knew we had some bad history, but I thought we'd overcome it.

Nerissa

I sat in the waiting room, feeling the thumping rhythm of my heart in my throat. When the surgeons finally came out, their somber expressions told me everything I needed to know. *No. Don't say it. Please don't say it.*

"Are you the family of Demario Barnes?"

"Yes. I'm his sister."

"I'm sorry, ma'am. We did everything we could, but your brother didn't make it," the doctor said gently.

My entire world shattered into a million pieces. I immediately broke down, my screeching sobs echoing through the hospital corridors. Everything from then on was one painful, grief-stricken blur. Somehow, I ended up in a hospital room bed with me and the baby being monitored until I was able to calm down. After what felt like an eternity, they confirmed that the baby was fine, and I was discharged.

Stepping outside the emergency room doors, I fumbled for my phone to call an Uber. As I swiped to the app, I saw Amir crossing the parking lot toward me. Rage immediately bubbled over inside me.

"I thought I told your ass to stay the fuck from around me!" I yelled, my voice filled with anger and grief.

Amir stopped in his tracks, his expression adamant. "You did. Hospital security threatened to call the police on my black ass if I came back too. But here I am."

My anger flared, and my emotions spilled over like lava from a volcano. "My brother's dead! He's dead!"

The moment the words flew out of my mouth, things became even more real. My rage slowly gave way to mind-blowing sorrow. I needed the hug, the support, and the feeling of not being alone now that the only family I had left was gone.

I was sixteen when my world shattered for the first time. My mother, my rock, was killed unexpectedly in a car accident. Losing her was a devastating blow, leaving me to navigate my unforgiving teenage years without my mother's guidance. Instead, I moved in with my father and had to grow up quickly, taking on household responsibilities far beyond my years while trying to sort through my grief.

A little over a decade later, just as I felt like I'd finally regained my footing, life dealt me another crushing blow, breaking me again—my father, who had been diagnosed with stage four pancreatic cancer. I watched helplessly as the disease quickly took its toll, especially being the only one there to carry the load of taking care of him while Demario served his time. Despite the stress, I remained by his side until he took his final breath. And now, Demario's death had only served as the next blow, reopening a wound that had never fully healed. His death had only left another deep scar next to my parents. I was so numb to death. All I could do was wail or sit in complete silence.

Amir stepped closer, closing the gap between us. I allowed him to wrap his strong arms around me. I cried rivers into his hard chest, my body rocking with sadness. He held me tightly, whispering soothing words while rubbing my back in slow circles. I slowly looked into his eyes and saw nothing but genuine concern. Still, I was numb to it all.

After a while, I pulled away and realized I was too distraught to go home alone. "I can't go home like this," I whispered.

Amir nodded, understanding. "Say less. Come with me. I'll take care of you."

He led me to his car and drove us back to the hotel he'd been staying at. As we entered his room, I felt a slight sense of relief. Despite everything, at least I wasn't alone, even if it did feel like I was sleeping with the enemy.

Amir gently guided me to the bathroom and drew me a warm bubble bath. Neither of us said a thing the entire time the water ran. All we did was watch the bubbles multiply in silence. He shut the water off and looked at me.

"Take your time," he said softly, leaving me to undress and soak underneath the soothing bubbles.

I FELT EXHAUSTED BUT SLIGHTLY MORE RELAXED WHEN I emerged from the bathroom. Amir approached me with a plate of food. While I was in the bath, he'd ordered room service, selecting a variety of dishes to ensure there was something I might want to eat. Little did he know, food was the last thing I wanted to see.

"You hungry?"

I scrunched up my nose, my appetite nonexistent. "No."

"C'mon, Nerissa. You need to eat for the baby's sake. At least try the fresh fruit," he urged gently.

"I can't, Amir. I just can't."

His expression softened. "Please, you need to eat."

When I refused, Amir took a strawberry and began to feed me, his patience unwavering. "Eat."

Eventually, I ate a few bites, more for the baby's sake than mine. Afterward, I curled up on the bed, and Amir lay beside me, pinning me close. Exhausted from all the crying, I soon fell asleep in his arms, but my slumber was far from peaceful. I was haunted by flashbacks of

Demario's death—the gunshots, the blood, the sirens. I woke up screaming and trembling.

Amir was still by my side. "It's okay, baby. I'm here. You're safe," he whispered, holding me tightly. As I calmed down, he kissed my forehead. "Until further notice, you're staying with me," he said firmly.

I didn't object. I was too weak and too damn overwhelmed to put up a fight about my rights and my freedoms. I simply nodded and allowed myself to lean on him as I thought about navigating the painful fucking days ahead.

Amir

Things were hard the week following Demario's death. After staying up all night watching over Nerissa as she slept, I woke up to an empty bed and an empty hotel room. She'd left me just like she did in Phoenix. Only this time, she'd sent a text explaining how she didn't want to see or talk to me while she was planning the funeral or for the foreseeable future after that. The only thing she wanted from me was space, which was the only thing I wasn't willing to give her. I was visibly fucked up over the fact that Nerissa thought I killed her brother or had a hand in hiring the one who did it. I hated that I couldn't change her mind. Maybe only time would tell. Perhaps it wouldn't. All I knew was I couldn't stand the thought of losing her again.

As I walked inside the dimly lit cigar bar to meet Ahsan, I pushed my thoughts about her to the side. The pungent aroma of smoke from various cigars filled the air. After scanning the room through the smoky haze, I found my brother seated in a cozy corner, sampling cigars for his upcoming wedding.

"Wassup?" I greeted him.

He reached out to dap me up with his free hand. "Sup?"

I sat beside him, and he passed me a fresh Cuban cigar to cut and puff on.

"So, what's going on with you and Nerissa?"

I shook my head, unwilling to get back in my feelings. "We shouldn't be talking about that right now. Tonight is about you and your wedding."

He took a deep breath. "Shit, there almost wasn't gonna be a fucking wedding."

I paused, almost choking on the smoke in my lungs. "What the fuck are you talking about, nigga?"

Ahsan took a deep puff. "I fucked up. I should've told Sienna about us keeping tabs on her bitch ass ex. And how he was siblings with your girl."

I raised an eyebrow. "Why didn't you?"

He sighed. "I didn't want to stress her out. She's already juggling enough with planning the wedding and attending art school. I thought I was protecting her, but now I feel like I just made shit worse."

"I get it, man. But why would she call off the wedding because of him?"

"It wasn't because of him. She just didn't want anything to happen at the wedding with so much shit going on, so she brought up calling it off. But don't worry. We're good now."

"How'd you get her to change her mind?"

His eyes were cold, almost menacing. "I told her the nigga was dead."

"Damn," I said, looking remorseful. "I'm sorry for dragging you into this messy shit."

He patted my shoulder. "It's all good. It all worked itself out."

My chest deflated with a slow exhale as cigar smoke curled from my nostrils. "Speaking of Demario, all the feelers I put out on his murder came back empty. The hit was clean. No loose ends."

"That's what you wanted, right?" he asked.

Before I could reply, my phone buzzed. It was XL calling from Miami. I answered and put the phone on speaker while leaning closer to Ahsan.

"Wassup?" I answered.

"Yo, I've still got eyes on this mothafucka Rico. He looks like he might be trying to run again. What's the move?"

"How do we know he didn't take out Demario?" Ahsan inquired.

"Nah. It wasn't. I've had eyes on him the entire time."

"You sure?"

"A hundred percent. His ass has been laying low for the most part. Someone else pulled that trigger."

I huffed, feeling my blood pressure elevate. "All right, move in on Rico. Bring him back to Vegas. We need to get answers."

"Got it. I'll keep you posted."

Half an hour later, I stepped out of the cigar bar, feeling tension and unease underneath my skin that I couldn't shake. The call from XL had left my nerves on edge. My trigger finger was itching, and I couldn't wait to introduce Rico to a bullet. As my legs propelled me down the street, my phone buzzed with a text from Sandra, the realtor. I glanced at it briefly, knowing my head was elsewhere, before shoving it back into my pocket without bothering to respond.

After getting inside my car, I couldn't bring myself to drive anywhere. Nowhere felt right without Nerissa. Not the hotel. Not my car. Not even in my own skin. Instead, I put on Kendrick Lamar's *Mr. Morale & The Big Steppers* album and drove until I found myself parked outside Jules's apartment. I spotted her by her car carrying a few grocery bags. My eyes narrowed as I watched her with disgust, being sure to keep a safe distance and not spook her too soon. She unlocked her apartment door, and her legs carried her inside, unaware I'd been watching her every move. I hung back, waiting until she was inside before calling the men I had stationed around the entrance and exits of her place.

"Call off the surveillance on Jules. Demario's dead. There's no more use for her."

My men acknowledged the order and left the apartment building. Once they were gone, I picked the lock to her front door with practiced ease, silently creeping inside. I looked around, surveying the space. The groceries she'd carried inside were still in the bags on the kitchen counter. Her keys were on the coffee table. I drifted down the hall, where her bedroom door was open. I heard the shower running. She hummed TLC's "Creep" softly to herself as she washed the day away without a care.

I sat on the edge of her neatly made bed, waiting. The minutes felt like decades as I listened to the sounds of her moving around, probably doing her nighttime routine or whatever bitches like her did when the sun went down.

Finally, she stepped out of the bathroom wrapped in a purple towel. Her eyes bulged in shock when she saw me sitting there.

She clutched her chest, visibly startled. "Amir? What the fuck are you doing in my place?"

"Demario's dead," I informed her.

Jules's brown face drooped as she stepped back, pressing her spine against her dresser. "W-what? H-how?"

I stood to my feet. "Doesn't matter how. What matters is, you're fuckin' next."

I lunged for her, violently snatching her throat in my grasp.

Her breath caught in her throat, fear dancing in her eyes. "Amir, w-why are y-you doing t-this t-to me? I-I thought you s-said y'all wouldn't h-hurt me."

"Consider it a lesson. Stay away from niggas who can get you killed."

Her eyes bulged as her nails dug into my forearms. I squeezed it like a fresh lemon on a hot summer day until I felt a pop under my gloved hands. As soon as her body hit the floor, I stood over her. A wave of peace washed over me. All but one of my looming threats had been handled. And as soon as XL returned to the city with Rico, I'd ensure the last of my enemies would be in the ground. After tucking her heavy, lifeless body underneath the covers, I headed for the door.

Nerissa

It was the day I'd been dreading since the moment the doctor told me my brother's heart was no longer beating. It was the day I'd have to say goodbye to Demario once and for all when we returned his body to the ground. The sky was overcast, matching my somber mood. A blur of people had come to pay their respects at the funeral. I stood by his graveside with tears rolling down my face. Amir was by my side like a shadow, offering silent support. No matter how many times I'd pushed him away since Maree took his last breath, Amir wouldn't stay gone. Even if I refused to open my front door to him, he'd bring me food or have my apartment guarded so that I'd feel "safe."

"I c-can't believe he's gone..." I whispered as I inhaled a stuttery breath.

I leaned into his shoulder, finding unspeakable comfort in his presence. He wrapped an arm around my waist, providing the strength I needed to stay collected.

"I'm strong," I choked out, barely above a whisper, saying it more for myself than for him.

He tipped his chin forward. "I know you are."

I stabilized. "I c-can take care of myself."

He caressed my shoulder. "I know, and you have."

I buried my tear-stained face in Amir's chest as he held onto me. All I could think about was how desperately I needed him. I needed his arms enveloping me. I needed him to rock me and whisper in my ear that I wasn't alone.

"I'm right here for you."

As the service concluded, people began to disperse from the cemetery. Air whizzed into my lungs as I tried to steady myself before turning away from the casket and going back to the car. I took a few faltering steps forward when I noticed a mysterious woman standing a little apart from the thinned-out crowd, watching the groundskeepers with a solemn expression on her face.

"I'll meet you at the car," I told Amir. I whisked myself over to the woman, my curiosity piqued and my nerves on ten. "Excuse me, but do I know you?"

She looked at me with a blend of sadness and hesitation. "No. But I'm sorry for your loss."

"How did you know my brother?"

"Me and D go way back. I used to date his cousin."

I paused as my eyes widened in surprise. "Hold up. Is your name Zyon?"

She gave a small, sad smile and nodded. "Yeah. How'd you know?"

"I overheard him on a phone call with you. I don't know what you're doing here, but you need to leave."

Her eyes widened. "Please, I didn't mean any disrespect. I just wanted to come and pay my respects to him and you."

"You don't need to show me shit but the back of your head when you leave this bitch!"

She waved her hands in surrender. "Please, again. I didn't mean any disrespect. It's just that D and I had an arrangement. He said he was coming back to town to leave something for me, and I wanted to know if he had mentioned anything to you about it before he passed."

"Are you seriously asking about money, and my brother's body isn't even in the fucking ground yet, bitch? I'm going to say this one time and one time only, so make sure you listen the fuck up! If you come sniffing around here for money again, I *promise* you I'll sing like a canary about your little secret," I warned her, my jaw tight with rage.

"Excuse me?"

I stepped closer. "I know you staged that robbery with my brother, and I know you don't want your cousin to find out. So if you don't stay your ass away, I'll bring hell right to your fucking front doorstep, *bitch*."

I stomped away, my heart pounding like a rabbit's as I turned back to Amir. He was waiting patiently by the car. All my bottled-up stress and grief had reared its ugly head. I didn't give a damn. As wound up as I was, it felt good to release my rage on someone who deserved it. I meant every last word too. I took Amir's hand, feeling a bit more at peace. It was the first time since Demario died that I felt like I could finally breathe again.

AMIR AND I LEFT THE REPAST. I STILL COULDN'T SHAKE THE weight of the day's events from my shoulders. I sat in the passenger seat and allowed him to drive me home. The car ride was filled with a comfortable silence, although I knew he had something on his mind. When we arrived, he walked me to my door.

"Do you need anything? Or want anything before I go?"

A breath eased out as I pushed my key into the lock. "The things I want, no amount of money can buy."

He took both of my hands in his, eyes burning with intensity. "Nerissa, I promise you, I had nothing to do with Demario's death. I would *never* do anything to risk losing you or our baby. I promised myself that I wouldn't let you get away again. So, if you wanna argue and tell me how much you hate me? You're still mine. You don't wanna speak to me and want your space? Fine. You're still mine. If there's ever a time you think you're not mine, just know you're *still* mine. And that's still my baby you carrying, and I ain't going nowhere."

I stood there, searching his sincere expression—his face, voice, and touch, the way he'd missed me and how serious he was about keeping me in his life. The lonely cavity of my ribs ached with every beat. I'd always had a sinking feeling in the pit of my stomach since the night he'd shown up at the emergency room. Deep down in my heart, I knew he didn't do it. And if he said he didn't, I had to make the decision to believe him.

"I don't hate you," I admitted, my voice barely a whisper against his chest.

"I know, Rizzy," he murmured, his arms tightening around my waist.

I looked up at him, my eyes brimming with tears. "But I *should* hate you. I want to."

"You *could* hate me, but I can't lie and say I'm not thankin' God right now that you don't."

"I don't want to lose myself in you, Amir. You're lethal to my heart."

"It's okay to be needy with me. I can give you everything you need, everything you want. We haven't even scratched the surface of what I have to offer."

I huffed. "I don't care about your money, Amir."

He cupped my face between his hands, his cognac-brown eyes sweltering with sincerity. "I'm not talking about the money, Rizzy. Fuck the money. I'm talking about my heart. And if you give me yours, I swear I'll drown myself in you."

I sighed. "I believe you, Amir," I said softly.

"Really?"

I nodded. "Yeah."

"What made you change your mind and decide to give me some grace?"

"That's what you do for the people you love, right?"

Just then, the baby kicked. Instead of waiting for his response, I placed Amir's hand on my belly, letting him feel the movement.

He smiled. "Wow, that's so wild."

"What do you think the baby's gender is?"

"I don't know, but I have a feeling it's going to be a surprise."

I shrugged. "I don't know. I think I might want to find out the sex before giving birth after all."

Amir dipped his chin before gathering me into his arms. "Whatever you decide, I'm with whatever you want."

Amir

Inside my hotel suite, the soft glow of candlelight flickered against the walls, setting the mood. The sounds of sappy R&B singers crooning one song after another played in the background as Nerissa and I enjoyed a relaxing bubble bath together. The tub was filled with fragrant bubbles and crimson rose petals. The soothing scent of lavender hung in the air. The moment was perfect, a realignment of our souls.

Holding her body close to mine in the warm water, I couldn't stop thinking about all we'd been through since reconnecting. Every minute I was around her, I felt a deep sense of gratitude for having her back in my life.

I gently caressed her baby bump, feeling the happy clicking of my heart. I was excited to meet our kid in a couple of months. "What do you think about the name Elijah for a boy?" I asked, my voice sounding soft as baby shit.

Rizzy smiled while leaning her curls back against my tattooed chest. "I like it. I'd call him Eli for short. You sure you don't want a junior?"

I shook my head. "Nah. I want my lil man to have his own identity in this world. I don't want him feeling like he will always be in my shadow."

"I get it. But what if it's a girl?"

My shoulders rose and fell. "I don't know. Something cute like Kyla."

"What do you think about the name Nimani or something short and sweet like Ava?" she suggested, her cocoa-brown eyes gleaming with a level of joy I hadn't seen on her in a while.

I'd missed how her smile lit up any room she walked into.

"I like Ava. What if we did Ava Nimani?" I proposed as my pruned fingertips skated up and down her wet skin.

"Ava Nimani, huh? It does sound kind of cute."

"Yeah. I think it does, too."

"I don't have my phone to write it down as a top contender. Can you reach yours?"

I nodded before reaching over the bathtub's edge to retrieve my phone. I texted Nerissa the first and middle name idea when, suddenly, my phone vibrated in my hand, breaking through our intimate bubble.

I groaned before glancing at the name on the screen and saw it was XL. I pushed out a quick huff through my nostrils before answering his call. "Hey, XL, what's up?"

XL's husky voice was urgent on the other end. "Amir, I just got back to Vegas. I need you to meet me at the warehouse."

My expression shifted from annoyance to concern, but I kept my voice calm. "All right, bet. I'll let you know when I'm on my way."

After ending the call, I looked down at Nerissa, who looked drowsy from the warm bath. "Who was that?"

I felt a pang of guilt in my chest. I hated leaving Nerissa, especially when we were finally reconnecting and back on good terms. But I knew I had to handle the Rico situation.

"My cousin. I have to step out for a bit, but I'll be back soon," I reassured her.

She nodded sleepily, her eyelids fluttering shut as she leaned against me. "Okay, be safe," she murmured.

Instead of making any sudden movements, I stroked her hair and watched her drift off to sleep. I kissed her forehead, carefully lifted her out of the tub, and wrapped her in a soft towel. I carried her to the bed and tucked her in gently before getting dressed and ready to go. Leaning down, I placed another soft kiss against her forehead.

"I love you," I whispered before quietly leaving the suite and heading to the warehouse. I hated leaving her but knew I had to handle my business.

I DROVE THROUGH THE NEON-LIT STREETS OF VEGAS, MY MIND racing with thoughts of Nerissa and the baby. The familiar sense of unease settled in my stomach as I approached the warehouse. I pulled a breath through my nostrils, trying to push aside the thoughts of Nerissa and focus on the task at hand. The warehouse was dimly lit, with eerie shadows snaking across the walls. I parked my car and stepped out with my pistol in hand. I marched toward the entrance, my footsteps echoing in the silence.

Inside, I found XL and Ahsan waiting for me with serious expressions etched across their faces. It was the moment of reckoning we'd all been waiting for.

"XL, what's going on?" I asked, my voice low.

He gestured toward the center of the room, where Rico was tied to a chair, his head hanging low. "You asked, and I delivered."

I stepped closer, scanning him from head to toe. A look of disgust passed over my features. His cocoa-brown skin was bruised and bloodied. His chin scraped his chest as his dreads swept over his damaged face. His clothes were ripped and bloodstained, signaling he'd put up a fight before surrendering. The sight of that nigga tied up and defenseless stirred up a tornado of emotions inside me— anger, disappointment, and a sense of retribution. Memories of Rico's past betrayals flooded the forefront of my mind. That mothafucka had caused me and my family so much trouble, and seeing him vulnerable, I couldn't help but feel a sense of fuckin' justice.

I traded glances with Ahsan, noticing the blood on his shirt and the bloodied hammer in his hand. I wasn't mad at him for getting his licks in. Besides, that nigga had betrayed us. He deserved every fucking thing he had coming to him. I stood before my opp, my eyes narrowing as I tried to quiet my raging dark thoughts. The room was tense, the silence only broken by the occasional creak of the warehouse structure surrounding us.

I grunted. "Wake his ass up."

XL punched him a few times until he coughed and spat out a mouthful of crimson blood. Rico groaned in agony.

I released the safety on my gun. "Don't waste no more of my time, nigga. Tell me what the fuck I want to know," I demanded, my voice cold and steady.

Rico slowly lifted his head, a menacing smirk playing on his bloodied lips despite his problematic situation. "You really don't know, do you?" he said, his voice dripping with disrespect. "This is all payback, mothafucka. And it's a bitch, ain't she?"

Ahsan's brow furrowed in confusion as he balled his fists. "Payback for what?"

"For what you did to my cousin, Kason!" Rico spat, his eyes blazing with anger. "You thought you could just take his life and get away with that shit, nigga? Nah. Not when it comes to my blood! So, I set you up to get back at you. It was me who took those shots at you. The only thing I regret is not putting your ass in the ground when I had the chance."

I felt a cold chill run down my spine. My brother had been set up and dragged into trouble, and now we all knew exactly why. The realization hit Ahsan hard as rage screwed up his face. He clenched his fists, struggling to keep his composure.

"You did all this shit to get back at me?" Ahsan asked, his voice low and dangerous.

Rico laughed bitterly. "An eye for an eye, right? Ain't that how the game go?"

"Nigga, fuck you and your bitch ass cousin! He fucked up when he put his mothafuckin hands on my girl at that hotel party. Anybody who touches her fucking dies, period!" Ahsan barked back.

I stepped back, giving Ahsan space to confront Rico however he saw fit. I planned to enjoy the show thoroughly. But before he could fly entirely off the rails, XL stepped up.

"So that's why you and Bradley ran when he was in the hospital? But we caught up to Bradley pretty quickly. Why'd you leave your man out to dry?" he inquired.

"The nigga wasn't supposed to get caught. But fuck him too. My loyalty is to my blood cousin who you murdered over some ho!"

Ahsan smacked his teeth, unable to hold his composure any longer. "Man, fuck this bitch ass nigga," he grumbled before swinging the hammer back like Thor and shattering Rico's kneecap.

Rico's cocky ass smirk quickly faded, replaced by a look of excruciating pain. He screamed. It was the type of high-pitched sound that made your eardrums bleed. No one wanted to have to experience that. Yet, here we were, watching the blood pour out of his knee like a waterfall. He'd learned the hard way that Ahsan wasn't to be fucked with, and the power dynamic took a hard shift.

"Were you ever working with Demario Barnes?" Ahsan probed.

"W-who the f-fuck is that?"

He drew back his arm again. "Answer the fucking question."

"I s-swear I don't know who the fuck that is. And even if I did, it wouldn't matter. I had no choice but to do what I did, nigga! You killed my family! We'll forever have beef behind that until one of us is six feet under. So, come on. Get on with it."

"Then I guess there's nothing else left for you to do but die, nigga." Ahsan growled before bashing the hammer into his skull.

I felt a sense of relief watching Rico take his last breath, but I couldn't shake the feeling that my relief was short-lived. XL stepped forward, his expression serious. "There's something else y'all need to know," he murmured.

Ahsan and I shifted our necks toward each other before looking at him with frowns creasing our foreheads. "What is it?" I asked first.

Instead of responding, XL gestured toward the warehouse door. "Come outside with me."

The three of us trekked outside into the night, the unspoken tension between us on a thousand. XL led us to his car and popped open the trunk. Inside, a woman was knocked out and bound by the wrists and ankles.

My heart somersaulted in my chest. "Who the fuck is she?"

"She was with Rico," XL explained. "She saw me when I went to get him, so I had to take her too."

Ahsan looked at the woman, then back at XL. "Is she dead?"

XL shook his head. "No, she's very much alive. For now."

I paused, trying to quickly process the situation as my mind galloped with possibilities. I knew we needed to act decisively. "Then you already know what you need to do," I said, my voice hardened.

XL nodded, understanding the gravity of the situation. "Yeah, I do."

"Good. Then it's settled."

Nerissa

Amir and I had become inseparable over the last few weeks. So much so that when he wasn't around, I craved him heavy. Not for sex but for his aura and his touch. It had been great connecting with him in nonsexual ways, but I couldn't wait to deliver our baby so that we could take our relationship to the *next* level. Most days, I could play it cool, but others, I wanted to feel every inch of his wood buried so deep inside me it felt like I was choking on dick.

I felt more connected and excited for the future as the days passed. My thoughts reflected on our journey and the foundation we'd managed to rebuild after crashing and burning the first time around. Lately, I'd never been more grateful for second chances. I loved how he secretly watched every move I made, how patient he was with me, and how he did everything in his power to put a smile on my face, even when he wasn't physically around. Additionally, I loved how he opened the car door for me and insisted on driving me to and from my weekly appointments.

I lay on the exam table with Amir beside me for my thirty-week doctor's appointment. I was excited to find out the sex of our baby and glad Amir hadn't given me any pushback on wanting to wait until delivery like I originally planned.

I spoke up just as the doctor placed the gel over my belly. "Dr. Reed, we've decided we want to find out the sex of our baby before my C-section," I said, my voice light with excitement.

She smiled warmly. "Of course. Let's take a look."

As the ultrasound began, the room fell so silent you could hear a pin drop. Moments later, Dr. Reed's face lit up with excitement. "Congratulations, it's a boy!"

Amir and I exchanged a look of pure joy. Tears welled up in my eyes as he leaned in to place a kiss on the top of my head. "A boy," he whispered in awe.

Joy rampaged my chest. *A son.* I couldn't believe it. I was going to be a boy mom. I cracked a soft smile, imagining the future moments I'd share with my little man. I thought about the unconditional love I'd exude for him and the lessons I'd teach. Yet, there was an unignorable layer of concern when it came to raising a black son in the world. I wondered where I'd fall between the mother I wanted to be and the mother I knew society would make me feel like I had to be. I didn't want to raise him out of fear, but most importantly, I didn't want to raise him alone.

I glanced up at Amir, and a little smile returned to my lips. I squeezed his hand. I hadn't felt more grateful for the sense of partnership and love I felt from him. Everything he'd said, he stood on, especially after finding out about the baby. Thinking about raising a son with him, I imagined the moments we'd share as a new family—the baby's first steps, the endless bedtime stories, the basketball games and karate matches. I couldn't wait to give our son the best possible upbringing in a home filled with love and promise.

After the appointment, we headed to the tailor to pick up Amir's tuxedo for his brother's wedding, which was only a few days away. The boutique was buzzing with activity, but we were in our own little bubble, still riding the high of the news that I was carrying a bouncing baby boy.

Amir tried on the custom-fitted black tuxedo, and I couldn't help but grin when he turned to face me. "How do I look?"

"You look handsome, best man," I replied with my hand resting on my globe-shaped belly.

He grinned while adjusting his gold bow tie in the mirror. "Just wait until our little man sees how fly we looked in these wedding photos someday."

I chuckled. "He'll probably think we're just as corny as we thought the adults were when we were growing up."

"I still can't believe we're having a boy."

"Me either. I think we should go through the list again and narrow it down now that we know."

He nodded thoughtfully. "All right, hit me with the top five contenders."

I opened up my notes app and read down my list. "Elijah, Ahmod, Amare, and Jhamir."

"Damn. I kinda like all of those, but we need to pick the one that feels right."

I grinned while stationing my gaze down at my belly. "What about Amare? It means eternal."

He paused, considering it for a moment. "Amare is nice. But what about Elijah? I still think that one is my favorite."

I sighed, weighing the pros and cons of each name in my mind. After a while, I gave up. "This is harder than I thought."

Amir chuckled before walking over and kissing the top of my head. "Yeah, but we'll figure it out. How about we pick our favorite and see if we can agree?"

I shrugged, ready to give it a go. "Okay, on three, all right?"

"Okay."

"One, two, three."

"Elijah," we both said at the same time, then burst into laughter.

"Well, I guess that settles it then," he stated with a grin. "Elijah, it is."

My cheeks bunched up with a grin. "Yeah. Elijah. I love it. Our baby Eli."

Amir wrapped his arms around me, pulling me close. "Me too. I can't wait to meet him."

"He'll be here before we know it," I confirmed. "Not soon enough if you ask me."

"Are you nervous about delivery?"

"Kind of. It's something I think about but I'm not dwelling on right now. I've been watching a million YouTube videos at night about different people's birth stories, trying to gauge how things could go. But you never know."

"Just know I'll be right there by you."

I spawned a smile of gratitude. "Thank you. So, now that you've got your tux for the wedding, where to next?"

"You wanna grab something to eat, then go shopping to pick up a few more things for the baby?"

I shrugged. "Yeah. Sure."

"Let me get changed, and then we can be on our way."

We left the shop with our fingers intertwined. From our unending conversations about middle names for the baby and nursery themes, it was clear that all we had on our minds was our son. For once, life felt ordinarily beautiful and full of love, with the bond of our future family growing tighter with each passing day. I couldn't help but imagine our future with baby Eli, feeling more connected and excited than ever.

WE SPENT THE NEXT FEW HOURS SHOPPING IN A BABY STORE packed with teeny-tiny clothes and cute toys. Of course, Amir went all out, picking up every cute outfit, tech gadget, and plush teddy he could find. I watched in amusement as the cart continued filling up, my brow furrowing as I realized how much he'd piled on. It was like déjà vu all over again.

Eventually, I couldn't help but ask, "Where exactly do you expect me to put all of this? My apartment is only so big."

He looked at me with a playful glint in his eyes and a mischievous grin. "I might have a remedy for that."

"What does that mean?"

Amir slipped his hand in mine as we headed toward the checkout counter. "You'll see." Once back inside the car, he turned to me and said, "I have a surprise for you."

I arched a questioning eyebrow. "Is this a surprise I'm going to like or hate?"

He smirked. "I guess we'll see."

With a gentle but firm hand, he blindfolded me. My heart gunned into overdrive, but I trusted him and went along with it. The car ride felt longer than it should've, and when we finally came to a stop, my anxiety was at an all-time high. He helped ease me out of the car before slowly removing the blindfold from my eyes. I blinked to see a beautiful single-family home standing before me.

My brows knitted together. "Whose house is this?"

"Ours," he replied, lacing his fingers with mine.

Surprise ran amok in my chest as I hesitantly followed him inside to find all my belongings already moved in. The open floor plan had high ceilings and sleek hardwood floors throughout the main floor, with oversized windows that allowed natural light to flood the space. The kitchen had a vast island, stainless steel appliances, and granite countertops. I barely had time to take it all in before he led me downstairs.

Shock unhitched my jaw as we descended to the basement, where my eyes landed on a fully equipped hair studio. There was a sleek salon chair, an oversized floor mirror, all my hair products, and even a neon sign that read "Nerissa's Glam Room" in vibrant pink above my workstation. I was speechless, my hand flying over my mouth.

"Are you fucking kidding me right now?"

"I wanted you to have a space where you can do what you love and be close to the baby," he said softly. "I know how much your work means to you."

My eyes welled up with tears of joy. "This is... so incredible. Thank you so much, Amir."

He pulled me into a gentle hug and then led me back upstairs. He stopped at the kitchen, pointing to the fridge. "Look at the fridge."

Underneath a cute heart magnet was an ultrasound image of our baby boy. I grinned with all my teeth. "I love this."

"C'mon, let me show you upstairs."

The master bedroom was spacious, with a king-sized bed and large bay windows framed with floor-to-ceiling curtains. Overhead was a beautiful chandelier with crystals hanging from the ceiling. There was a sitting area by the window, a spacious walk-in closet, a master bathroom with a clawfoot tub, a glass shower, and a double vanity with sleek marble countertops.

Amongst the other bedrooms upstairs was an almost fully set-up nursery. The room was painted a soft, pastel yellow, and the bright sun rays streamed through the windows. A plush rocking chair sat in the corner, waiting for those late-night feedings. Next to it was the changing table, already stocked with a pack of diapers. It was a warm and inviting space that was perfect for welcoming the newest member of our family. All that was left to put together was the crib. We stood there, surrounding the open crib box.

Tears gummed up my throat. "Amir, I—I can't believe you did all this."

He shot his gaze down to the open box, revealing the pieces of a white crib. "The movers wanted to put the crib together, but I said I wanted to be the one to do that. I figured it shouldn't be too hard, right?" he asked with a chuckle.

I snickered as I drifted over and picked up the instruction manual from the dresser. "Famous last words. Let's see... Step one says to attach the, uh, side panels to the base."

He looked at all the pieces in the box with confusion etched in his expression before grabbing two and attempting to screw them together.

"Are you sure that's the right way?" I probed, tilting my head as I looked at the unassembled crib before rechecking the instructions.

Amir nodded confidently. "Yeah, I'm pretty sure. If not, we'll just have to take this bitch apart and start over again."

After a few hours of working together and laughing through our confusion as we figured out what went where, the crib was finally assembled. We stepped back to admire our handiwork, knowing damn well we *never* wanted to build another crib again.

"What do you think?" Amir asked.

I placed a hand on my belly. "It looks good! I think Eli is going to love it."

Amir wrapped an arm around my shoulders. "Yeah, he will. And just think, soon he'll be sleeping right here."

"This is really happening," I said softly. "We're going to be somebody's parents."

He dipped his chin before pulling me into a hug. "Yeah, we are. And we're going to be the best at it."

I looked around the room, feeling a sense of accomplishment. "I still can't believe you bought us an entire fucking house, Amir. Like, who does that?"

"You can't tell me you weren't getting tired of laying up underneath me in that hotel or your small ass apartment."

"You're not wrong about that."

Amir stationed his eyes on mine, his gaze soft as silk. "Besides, you deserve to have a home, not just a house, Nerissa. I want us to be a family."

Before I could respond, he kneeled on one knee while pulling out a ring from his pocket. I immediately went misty-eyed as I tried to catch my breath through my rapid-fire heartbeats. My lips flopped apart. As badly as I wanted to say something, all I could do was stand there with my knees knocking together.

He continued. "Nerissa, I never should've let you get away the first time. You being back in my life is something I don't take for granted. I meant it when I told you that you were mine, Nerissa. My heart is yours, and so am I. I'm in love with you. My whole being is wrapped around you. Nothing is ever going to change that. I want to show you that I'm ready to be the man you've always needed me to be for you and myself. All I need is you by my side as my wife. I'm not asking you this because I feel pressured or because it's the right thing to do. I'm asking you to be my wife because I can't live without you, Nerissa Barnes. Will you marry me?"

My eyes closed for a lengthy blink. Tears squeezed from the corners, chasing one another down my cheeks. His proposal slackened the tension in my jaw. *Is this real? Is he asking me to marry him?*

I pinched myself. I wasn't dreaming. Everything was real.

I bit my lip to contain my tears as my chin descended in a nod. "Y-yes. I will."

A smile ruffled his lips as he slid the diamond ring on my finger before pushing himself to stand. "I love you."

"I love you too."

Amir

The sun shone brightly as we gathered in front of Ahsan's newly completed mixed-use building. The tall, sleek building housed residential apartments on the upper floors and bustling small black-owned businesses ready to open on the ground level, one of them being XL's soul food restaurant. I couldn't help but feel proud as I stood a few feet away, watching them prepare to cut the ribbon.

Applause erupted around us as Ahsan snipped the red ribbon. I twinned my brother's broad smile as I leaned in and gave him a hearty hug. "Congrats, bro! This shit is incredible!"

Ahsan beamed with pride. "Thanks, man. I couldn't have done it without everybody's support."

I pulled XL in for a hug next, excited for his second business endeavor. "And congrats to you, too, cuz. I know the line is going to be wrapped around the building the day you open!"

XL stroked his beard as he grinned from ear to ear. "Thanks, fam. I know Big Mama is smiling down on her boys right now."

Ahsan's lips danced around a smile. "It's like you can feel it, right?"

I nodded in agreement. "Hell yeah," I agreed.

XL cracked a sly grin while reaching out to dap us up. "Ain't no stoppin' them Patton boys."

"So, about your wedding next week," I started with a playful grin. "What were you thinking, having a grand opening a week before your wedding?"

Ahsan laughed, shaking his head. "I know, I know. Timing's a bit crazy, but as you can see, everything's falling into place, nigga."

"You know we always land on our feet," XL added.

My brother let amusement flow through him before his face went serious. "Now, let's talk business. How are things progressing under your leadership?"

I worked up a cocky grin. "We've officially expanded into Texas. I'm flying to Chicago in the next few weeks to meet with a new potential connect to talk about expanding into the Midwest. It's a huge step for us."

He clapped me on my back. "That's wassup. You've outdone yourself."

"Thanks," I said, then hesitated momentarily before continuing. "There's something else I wanted to tell y'all. I asked Nerissa to marry me, and she said yes."

XL's eyes crinkled with a smile as he pulled me into a quick hug. "Oh shit! Congratulations to both of you!"

My brother's eyes widened in surprise and joy. "Congrats, yo. I knew she was the one."

"Oh, you did?"

"Yeah."

I cocked my head to the side. "How?"

"Look at you, nigga. It's like you grew up overnight. It took the right woman to bring that shit out of you. I'm proud of you, Amir. It's only up from here."

Emotion stirred behind my eyes. I couldn't describe how it felt to have my brother tell me how proud he was of me. "Thank you, bro."

"Looks like we have even more to celebrate," XL said.

"That's what Ahsan's bachelor party is for, right?"

Ahsan bit back a grin. "I trust you with the bachelor party. Just... keep that shit somewhat sane, all right?"

I winked. "Don't worry, nigga. I'll make sure you get down that aisle, even if I have to drag you there myself."

One week later.

As the sun began to set, spreading a golden glow over the rooftop, I stood in front of the mirror, adjusting my gold bow tie. I looked good as fuck in my black tuxedo. I glanced at Ahsan, the groom, who was getting a last-minute shape-up from XL. His wedding was set to start in less than an hour, and the space was overflowing with excitement and nerves. I decided to pour three shots of Henny for a moment of calm before the ceremony kicked off. I handed a shot glass to each of them before raising mine to toast Ahsan.

"Today is your big day, bro. Here's to you and the love of your life."

We clinked our glasses together and downed the shots, feeling the warmth spread through us.

Then, I pulled out a box of cigars and handed one to Ahsan and XL, lighting each one. The room filled with the pungent aroma of the Cuban cigars as we took our first puffs.

"Yo, I can't believe this day is finally here," Ahsan said, exhaling a cloud of smoke.

"You're doing this shit. You're marrying the love of your life," I confirmed.

Ahsan smiled, and I caught a glimpse of joy and nerves in his eyes. "Yeah, it's surreal. But I couldn't have done it without you niggas. Y'all have always had my back."

XL chimed in. "We're family. That's what we do. And today, we're here to celebrate you and your future wifey."

I placed a hand on Ahsan's shoulder. "You've got this. I know I initially gave Sienna a hard time, but she's amazing, and everyone knows you two are perfect for each other."

"Just remember to breathe and enjoy every fucking moment of today," XL added.

Ahsan nodded, taking a deep breath. "Thanks, y'all. I'm ready."

We shared a moment of silence, savoring the camaraderie and the significance of our bond as a family. I looked at my brother with admiration evident in my eyes. "Now, let's get your black ass down that aisle."

With that, we finished our cigars, took one last look at each other, and headed out to the ceremony, ready to embrace the next chapter.

AHSAN AND SIENNA'S WEDDING CEREMONY HAD BEEN NOTHING short of beautiful. The intimate setting, with the Vegas skyline as a backdrop at sunset, was perfect. I watched my brother exchange vows with his bride and couldn't help but think about Nerissa. My thoughts raced with excitement as I smiled, imagining the day she'd walk down the aisle to me and the joy of welcoming our son into the world in a couple of months. Every time I looked at her, I knew I was committed to loving and cherishing her for the rest of my life. I knew that marriage would bring its own challenges, but I was ready to face them all with Nerissa by my side.

During the reception, I took the microphone to make my toast. The crowd hushed as I tapped the side of my glass.

"Ladies and gentlemen, could I please have your attention? First, I'd like to thank everyone for being here to celebrate Ahsan and Sienna. For those who don't know me, I'm Amir, the proud best man and even prouder baby brother of the groom. Ahsan, standing here today, I can't help but remember the countless memories we shared growing up under Big Mama's wing. With all the shit we got into as kids, you've always been my rock. But seeing you with Sienna, I see a side of you that I never knew existed. She brings out the best in you. And to Sienna, you are everything my brother has ever needed and more. I couldn't be happier to welcome you into the Patton family. I think I speak for everyone here when I say that you two are an unstoppable duo. I wish y'all nothing but endless love. So, let's raise our glasses to the newlyweds, Mr. and Mrs. Ahsan Patton. Cheers!"

As I raised my glass of champagne, I noticed Sienna was holding a glass of sparkling water instead. It struck me as odd, but I didn't dwell on it at the moment. Later that evening, my curiosity somehow got the better of me. I pulled Ahsan aside and asked him about her drink selection. It was her wedding reception, after all. Everybody should've been turnt the hell up.

Ahsan looked at me and doubled his smile before leaning in. "She's pregnant. We were gonna wait until after the wedding to tell everybody."

My eyes widened with joy as I reached out to hug my brother tightly. "Congrats, bro!"

"Thank you. It's early, but we're both excited."

It was a moment of pure celebration, knowing that Ahsan was on the way to starting his own family and relishing in his happily ever after.

As the reception's festivities continued, Nerissa and I occupied the photo booth in the corner, capturing silly moments with the props. When it was time to cut the cake, Ahsan and Sienna playfully fed each other slices of their three-tier cake before she smashed some into his face. I captured the moment on my phone, knowing we'd relive those laughs forever. As the evening progressed, an unrehearsed dance-off broke out on the dance floor. Ahsan, known for his dance moves, led the charge and had everyone cheering and shaking their asses, keeping the party going until the venue shut down.

Those special moments and the announcement of Sienna's pregnancy made my brother's wedding reception a night I'd never forget. I couldn't help but feel grateful to be part of such a celebratory milestone and looked forward to hitting my own with my growing family.

Nerissa

S*ix weeks later.*

I sat in the hospital room, my heart pitter-pattering in my chest with a fusion of excitement and nerves. Today was the day I would meet my baby boy. Amir held my hand tightly, his presence a comforting anchor in the sea of my feelings.

"I'm so nervous," I confided to Amir.

"You're going to do great," he whispered, his voice reassuring.

I nodded, trying to focus on his words rather than the fluttering behind my ribcage. The doctors had scheduled my C-section, and while I trusted them, the thought of lying on a table and being cut into had my anxiety at an all-time high.

As they wheeled me back into the operating room, Amir stayed rooted by my side, gowned from head to toe, and never letting go of my hand. I noticed the operating table in the center of the bright, sterile space. Goosebumps raised on my skin, reacting to how cold the room was. Despite the thumping rhythm in my throat, I felt a sense of peace wash over me. Soon enough, we'd meet our baby boy.

My doctor and her medical team worked swiftly, and soon, I felt a gentle tugging sensation and some pressure. Moments later, the room was filled with the most beautiful sound I'd ever heard—the sweet cry of our newborn son. Tears of joy escaped from the corners of my eyes as the nurse brought the baby over to me.

"He's perfect," Amir confirmed, his voice choking with emotion as he swiped a tear from his eye.

His emotional reaction only amplified the joy spreading throughout my body, making it an unforgettable moment. I gazed at our son, soaking in everything about him—from his ten tiny fingers and toes to his long eyelashes and head full of soft dark curls. His little finger tightly coiled around mine, and the first time he looked into my eyes, it took my breath away. He looked just like his father.

"Hi, Elijah. I'm your mommy."

Tears of happiness streamed down my face as I held Elijah close. I knew that every bit of anxiety leading up to that moment had been worth it. I was suddenly overwhelmed with a rush of emotions. I was a mother. With Amir by my side and our healthy, handsome baby boy safe in my arms, I felt like I could take on the world.

"I love you," Amir said while stroking the top of my head with his thumb.

A smile breezed over my lips. "I love you, too."

____

AHSAN

SIENNA AND I RUSHED INTO THE HOSPITAL. I FELT A BLEND OF excitement and nerves fluttering around inside my chest. I'd been eagerly awaiting the day for months. As Sienna and I entered the maternity ward, we were greeted by the welcoming grins of the nurses. I quickly found my way to the waiting room, where XL and Amir were gathered. I exchanged hugs and daps with them, who were both equally excited. Amir beamed his gratitude as he announced that Nerissa had given birth to a healthy baby boy, and they were both doing okay.

"We named him Elijah," Amir confirmed. "C'mon, let's go see him."

I repaid my brother's grin with one of my own. I couldn't wait to meet my nephew for the first time. He led us to Nerissa's room, where she was resting with the newborn in her arms. After washing my hands, I approached my brother, who stood beside her, gazing at his son with awe.

I felt a rush of emotions, which prompted me to give him another big hug. "Congratulations, bro! You're a father now. He's perfect."

"Oh my God! He's so handsome. I'm so happy for you two!" Sienna said, standing at my side.

XL added, "Welcome to the world, little man. You've got a big family that loves you so much already."

Amir, with tears in his eyes, brought a smile to bear. "Thanks, y'all."

Nerissa looked up at us, visibly exhausted but still glowing with joy. "Do you want to hold your nephew, Ahsan?"

I locked a grin on him as she gently handed my nephew to me. "We need all the practice we can get."

Holding my newborn nephew for the first time, an unexpected sensation swept over me. I couldn't help but marvel at his delicate features—his tiny fingers, his soft caramel skin, the peaceful expression on his face as if he didn't have a care in the world. As I cradled my nephew, my thoughts drifted to my unborn daughter. I couldn't help but imagine holding her for the first time in a few more months and feeling her tiny heartbeat against my bare chest. Elijah's little life had stirred up something deep inside me. It was then that I knew everything I'd done that had led us to that moment was worth it.

My actions had haunted me for months, replaying in the back of my mind like on an endless loop. I was the one who'd pulled the trigger and killed Demario. He was a threat to my brother's family and mine. The thought of the people I loved suffering or being in danger was unbearable, and I would do anything to keep them safe. After Sienna confronted me about not telling her everything about Demario and his connection to Nerissa, she threatened to call off the wedding until everything blew over. I couldn't have that shit. The nigga had to be dealt with. So, I was the one who sat outside Nerissa's apartment and took him out.

I glanced over at Amir, who still hadn't let go of the smirk on his lips. I'd never seen him happier. Happiness looked good on him. I wanted my brother's hands to be clean for the sake of his new family. And because of my actions, they were. The secrecy had been eating away at me, but I vowed never to tell a soul, knowing that spilling the truth would only bring more harm. I looked around the room filled with the closest people to me. Whenever doubt crept in about what I'd done, I reminded myself of my family's well-being. I did what I did for them; if it came down to it, I'd do it again.

THE END

Afterword

A note from K.L. Hall.

Reader,

Thank you for reading *Gimme a Gangsta: The Patton Brothers Book Two*. If you've made it this far, I hope you'll consider telling me what you thought about the book in the form of a **five-star review and/or rating**. Don't hesitate to let me know what you'd like to see from me next! I thoroughly enjoy reading your thoughts and hearing from you as well! I'm always striving to attract new readers and retain current ones, and reviews are one of the easiest ways to attract readers. If you loved the book, tell a friend, and most importantly, let me know!

All my love,
K.L. Hall

About the Author

K.L. Hall is a national bestselling and award-winning author. As a serial storyteller, Hall has penned over three dozen titles in various genres—including African American urban fiction and romance, paranormal, children's books (as Kimberley M.), and non-fiction. Her fictional stories straddle the intersection of classic Urban and spellbinding Romance.

Highly Acclaimed Titles:

In the Arms of a Savage: (Peaked at #1 in Women's Fiction)

The Potomac Falls Series (Peaked at #1 and #2 in African American Erotica)

Sign up for my mailing list to stay updated with new releases, giveaways, sneak peeks, and more! Click this link: https://bit.ly/38RMpV5

Connect with me on social media:

Facebook: https://www.facebook.com/authorklhall

Twitter: https://twitter.com/authorklhall

Instagram: https://www.instagram.com/officialklhall/

Website: https://www.authorklhall.com

Other novels by K.L. Hall:

Diary of a Hood Princess 1-3

Rise of a Street King: The Justice Silva Story (*Spin-Off to the Diary of a Hood Princess series*)

Broken Condoms and Promises 1-3

In the Arms of a Savage 1-3

Built for a Savage: Blaze and Camille's Love Story (*Spin-Off to the In the Arms of a Savage Series*)

A Ruthle$$ Love Story 1-3

Fallin' for the Alpha of the Streets 1-2

The Most Savage of Them All: The Wolfe Calloway Story (*Prequel to the In the Arms of a Savage Series*)

When a Gangsta Loves a Good Girl

Caught Between My Husband and a Hustler

The Illest Taboo 1-2

To the Only Thug I'll Ever Love

A Lover's Heist: Chief and Gianna's Love Story

A Lover's Heist II: Rome and Lira's Love Story

A Lover's Heist III: Baby and Skai's Love Story

Crushed Velvet & Cashmere

Crushed Velvet & Cashmere 2

Entanglements

Never Had a Bad Boy Love Me So Good

Good Girls Always Got a Thing for the Thugs

Professor Zaddy: A Potomac Falls Novel

Bound in the Arms of a Thug: Chop & Kendyl's Love Story

Make Mine a Gangsta: The Patton Brothers Book One

Gimme a Gangsta: The Patton Brothers Book Two

Short Reads + Novellas:

Bi-Curious: An Erotic Tale

Bi-Curious 2: Tastes Like Candy

A Savage Calloway Christmas (*Christmas novella to the In the Arms of a Savage Series*)

Lovin' the Alpha of the Streets: A Valentine's Day Novella (*Valentine's Day novella to the Fallin' for the Alpha of the Streets Series*)

Awakened: A Paranormal Romance

As Long as You Stay Down

Solace in Seven

Solace II: The Final Cut

Something Bleu

Something Borrowed

Something New

The Knight Before Christmas: A Potomac Falls Short

I'll Be Home for Christmas: A Potomac Falls Short Book II

Triggered: A Potomac Falls Novella

Wasted Off You: A Friends to Lovers Novella

Because You Don't Know My Name: A Potomac Falls Novella

Will You Say My Name: A Potomac Falls Novella Book Two

Remember My Name: A Potomac Falls Novella Book Three

Every Thug Needs a Lady: A Lady and the Tramp Retelling

Ten Things I Hate About Lovin' You: An Enemies to Lovers Novella

In Exchange: An Urban Thriller

T.A.N.: An Erotic Novella

Children's Books:

Princess for Hire

Princess Twinkle Toes & the Missing Magic Sneakers

Little One, Change the World

Adjust Your Crown: A Self-Love Coloring Book for Children of Color

Non-Fiction:

Authors are a Business: The Booked & Busy Course Mini Book

BLP

Visit bit.ly/readBLP to join our mailing list for sneak peeks and release day links!

Let's connect on social media!
Facebook - B. Love Publications
Twitter - @blovepub
Instagram - @blovepublications

We hate errors, but we are human! If the B. Love team leaves any grammatical errors behind, do us a kindness and send them to us directly in an email to blovepublications@gmail.com
with ERRORS as the subject line.

As always, if you enjoyed this book, please leave a review on Amazon/Goodreads, recommend it on social media and/or to a friend, and mark it as READ on your Goodreads profile.

By the Book with B Podcast: bit.ly/bythebookwithb